CW01220127

DEADLY CARGO

A Chase Adams FBI Thriller

Book 13

Patrick Logan

First Edition: February 2024

DEADLY CARGO

Patrick Logan

Prologue

THE TRUCK DRIVER WIPED SWEAT from his brow. It was hot, and the sun filtering in through the windshield was bright. The cab was air-conditioned, and even though the vehicle was long past its prime, he could still feel cool air pumping through the vents.

And yet, he was forced to continually wipe sweat from his eyes and forehead every few seconds. The front of his T-shirt—he'd long since removed and tossed aside the flannel shirt he'd been wearing over top—was soaked from the collar to the small of his back.

The man reached for the bottle of water in the cup holder, put it to his lips, and then frowned.

It was empty.

He shook the plastic as if trying to make more liquid appear out of nothing, and then ran his tacky tongue over the surface, dipping it inside several times in an attempt to salvage any and every last drop.

The man threw the bottle onto his flannel shirt and then aimed his eyes at the road ahead.

"Shit!" he shouted, yanking the wheel to the left. He heard the cargo shifting in the back, culminating with a hard thump on the thin wall separating the cab from the trailer.

For the entire two hours he'd been driving on the winding mountain pass, he'd not seen a single car.

He hadn't seen much of anything, in fact. Just dirt and gravel and dust.

Until now.

In the center of the road was a large, female Lynx. Its mottled fur, patchy and thin, seemed almost too large for its frail body, highlighting the desperation in its eyes.

As the 18-wheeler swerved to avoid running the animal over, the driver saw two cubs nestled against its bony ribs.

He pressed the brake hard, and the cab lurched forward, the truck's tires struggled to gain traction on the soft road.

Again, there was a thud behind, this time accompanied by a low moan.

It could have been the worn brake pads protesting the heat or it could have been something else entirely.

Either way, it took a good twenty yards before the truck came to a complete stop. And when it finally did, the man sat with his hands firmly planted on the wheel, his breathing heavy and shallow.

That was close, he thought. *That was* really *close.*

The man, slowly recovering from the shock, moved his eyes from the windshield to the driver-side window.

"What the hell?"

The lynx was gone, as were the cubs.

The man whipped his head around rapidly, trying to figure out where it could have possibly gone. The animals were notorious for blending into their surroundings, as well as being lightning quick, but there was nowhere to hide on this road. Come to think of it, there was nowhere to come or go, either.

Had it gotten lost? It looked sick—maybe not feral, but definitely malnourished. Maybe it had gotten confused and wandered down from one of the mountains and was too disoriented to find its way back to its nest.

The man continued to glance around, and as he did, he felt pressure building behind his eyes.

He chalked this up to dehydration.

Why didn't I grab more water at the last truck stop? He cursed his own stupidity. And then he cocked his head. *Is there water in the back?*

No, just keep going. You don't have time to stop.

He had a delivery to make, several of them, in fact. But the last thing he wanted to do was run the animal over. Not because he cared about the mangy Lynx's safety, but blowing a tire or snapping an axle would spell disaster. It wasn't as if he could just call AAA.

The man who had hired him had made the rules explicitly clear. Nobody, including him, was to look in the back of the truck until the first delivery. And even then, it was best if he averted his eyes.

He knew the drill. Don't ask questions, just mind your own fucking business, and do your job.

Simple.

The second rule was that all deliveries must be made or none of the significant sums of money he'd been promised would ever find his bank account.

His mind immediately went to drugs. And if he was transporting narcotics, then a little bump might be all he needed to get rid of this damn headache and keep him awake.

No—don't fuck this up, he scolded himself.

Still, running over the Lynx would be a nightmare. Arriving at the first stop with blood and intestines trailing behind him would only raise questions.

His employer didn't strike him as a man who liked questions.

The driver reached into the glove box and pulled out a pistol. It was old, nearly as worn as ancient as the truck itself, but it would be more than sufficient to scare off a sick Lynx.

He grabbed the door handle but then stopped when his head suddenly exploded with pain. This was unlike the dull throb of a headache he'd had for at least the past hour. This was a lightning bolt inside his skull.

What the actual fuck?

The pain was so intense that his vision blurred. Once, during a similar delivery, his truck had broken down in the middle of nowhere. It had been nearly eight hours before someone found him. He'd been dehydrated then, his piss thick like maple syrup. It was also a similar shade of brown.

This was not that.

The man clenched his jaw and opened the door.

Can't stop… need to make… deliveries…

His headache worsened the instant the bright sunlight flooded his eyes.

"Here… kitty… cat. Here… cat…" His words were staccato. Even thinking them proved difficult.

He waved the gun in front of him as he shuffled along the length of the unmarked truck.

"Where did you go?"

The man dropped his considerable belly to the ground and peered underneath the truck.

No Lynx.

Where the fuck *did you go?*

It was a struggle to get back up again and twice the man thought about just rolling beneath the trailer for a nap.

Just a short… cat nap.

He laughed.

It hurt.

It might just have been a mirage, the man thought. *God damn it, I'm so* fucking *thirsty.*

Convinced that wherever the animal had gone, if there, indeed, had been an animal at all, it wouldn't ruin his truck, he started back toward his open door.

Then he heard something.

A distinct thump.

The man's movements were labored as he went to investigate, thoughts of *don't ask, don't tell* buried beneath the throbbing in his head. Every time he lifted his leg, hell, every heartbeat caused more blinding pain.

The dust was messing with his breathing, making him wheeze.

Without thinking, he unlatched the rear doors and lifted the lever. And then he jumped back as something inside the truck pushed its way out.

A zombie.

A *fucking* zombie.

Red eyes, swollen, pock-marked cheek, a single hand ending in tetanic digits outstretched.

"Fucking hell!" he shouted.

The zombie took one step and then fell to the ground, sending a giant puff of dirt into the air.

With that same twisted hand, it tried to drag itself forward.

The driver watched in horror as the thing's entire body seemed to tense.

And then it went still.

Forgetting all about the gun, the man's eyes lifted from the fallen corpse to the back of the trailer.

And then he screamed and ran.

There were more of them in there.

At least five, but there could have been dozens or even hundreds waiting in the shadows.

Begging for him to come closer.

No way. No fucking *way.*

He didn't care how much he was being paid or if there was a rabid Lynx roaming the area.

He ran as hard as he could.

Despite his determination, the man only made it about a hundred yards before something in his head exploded. His vision bloomed red and then he collapsed.

The man was dead before he hit the ground his last thought incomprehensible.

They're going to get me. Then they're going to kill me and consume my flesh.

PART I – Seven Bodies

Chapter 1

I HATE YOU, CHASE ADAMS.

The thought came out of nowhere, and it lingered.

I hate you, Chase Adams.

"Hurry up! We gotta go!" Chase hollered.

Tate Abernathy cursed, lowered his chin to his chest, and pumped his arms and legs even faster.

He despised running. He loathed it nearly as much as he loathed Chase Adams.

She'd lied to him.

After everything they'd been through and the countless times they'd promised each other to tell the truth, she was nothing but a boldfaced liar.

She told him—no, not told him, but *assured* him, that the first few times he went on a run, it would hurt, and it would suck. But after a while, he'd grow to enjoy it.

Yet, after nearly three full years of running a minimum of two times a week, but usually three or four, he didn't enjoy it at all.

If anything, he hated it more now than ever.

Tate lifted his eyes and swiped his bare arm across his forehead.

Chase was already home, standing on the front porch of their shared three-bedroom townhouse. What made everything worse was that look on her face.

She was actually smiling.

Using his hatred as fuel, Tate finished the run and then put his hands on his knees and bent at the waist. He felt like puking, and almost did, only that wasn't possible; he needed to catch his breath first.

The feeling eventually passed and, still doubled over, he glanced up at Chase. He stared into her sparkling green eyes and said the words that he'd been thinking for the entirety of the five-mile run: "I hate you."

Chase threw her head back and laughed.

He didn't understand how she was barely breathing heavily while he was at death's door. Chase looked fresh, her pretty face a healthy pink.

"Shut up," she said. "You love me."

Tate opened his mouth to refute this claim, but instead, spat something that looked almost alive onto the ground.

"Gross," Chase said, putting a hand on his back and helping him to stand. "Now, come on, we don't have much time. Get showered up."

Oh, how I despise you, Chase Adams.

***

Tate hated to run, but there was no denying that all this exercise was having a positive effect on his body.

The paunch that he typically held around his waist, the thickness to the back of his arms, and the little bit of extra skin hanging from his chin was all but gone now. He would never be an *Instagram* model, nor did he have any aspirations to become one. But at nearly 50 years old, Tate couldn't help but think that he was in the best shape of his life.

Sure, he had more gray in his hair at the temples than ever before, and his mustache, which he kept trimmed short, was now more salt and pepper than oak colored.

But he didn't mind.

Neither did Chase; she told him that it made him look distinguished—a euphemism for old if there ever was one.

But at least Tate didn't *feel* old.

Unless he was running. When he was running, Tate felt like a geriatric man in desperate need of both hip and knee replacements.

Tate shaved his chin and cheeks, and then put some cream on his face, part of a simple skin care regimen that Chase had introduced him to and encouraged.

"Dad? We're going to be late!" Rachel yellow from below.

"Tate, hurry up!" Georgina reiterated.

"I'm coming," Tate grumbled. "I'm coming."

He quickly retreated to his room and got dressed in what everyone referred to as his uniform: a pair of dark slacks, a white button-down with a soft collar, and an unstructured blazer.

Like his diet, his exercise regime, and his skin care routine, Chase had attempted to change his style, too. She wanted him to wear jeans more often and if he was dead set on a shirt with a collar, to switch to polos.

He declined.

After all, he had to put his foot down somewhere.

Tate found everyone waiting in the front hall and was struck by how much they looked like a real family. After the car accident that had seen his then-wife Robin convicted of a crime she didn't commit and Rachel being paralyzed from the waist down, he thought that things would never get better.

Fast forward a couple of years and his life was almost unrecognizable. While his ex-wife was still incarcerated, he'd met someone, someone for whom the love he felt rivaled that of the feelings he'd had for Robin when they first met. And, after innumerable physiotherapy appointments—damned expensive appointments that weren't covered by the FBI's shitty health plan—Rachel had managed to rebuild and repair some of the neural pathways that had been damaged. She wasn't one hundred percent, not close to it, and he doubted that she ever would be. But he was damn proud of his daughter. Rachel had made so much progress that she'd lost the need for her wheelchair entirely and now relied on poles with wrist attachments to get around.

Then there was Georgina Adams.

When he'd first met the girl, he'd immediately pegged her as an intelligent, smart-mouthed, witty, and well-adjusted young girl. She had fiery red hair and perhaps the most intense green eyes that he'd ever seen. Her hair was the same color now, but her look had matured significantly. Georgina Adams, like her aunt, had always been good-looking, in a cute sort of way. But now, as she entered her middle teens, Georgina was bordering on beautiful. In a few years, she would be drop-dead gorgeous.

"What are you smiling at?" Chase asked, her brow furrowing.

Ah, Chase.

Always in exceptional shape, she almost seemed to be aging backward, a real-life Benjamin Button.

Except for her hair.

Tate often complained about the white in his mustache and on his head, but Chase never did. It was difficult to describe the exact shade of her shoulder-length hair. It wasn't white, not exactly, not like that of a prestigious elderly woman.

It was more… an absence of color. Over the years, Chase had tried to dye it many times. But no matter how good a job the hairdresser did, she always ended up reverting back to her natural shade—or lack thereof.

And Tate liked it. She might placate him with claims that his own salt-and-pepper look made him appear distinguished—*old*—but with Chase, her hair color added an element of mystery.

"I was just thinking—"

"Well, do your thinking later," Rachel snapped. "We're gonna be late and I don't want to be the last person to arrive at Virginia Tech. It's bad enough that you insist on driving me when everyone else is just taking the bus or carpooling. Don't be cringe, dad."

"I—"

Chase leaned over and kissed him on the cheek.

"Yeah, dad," she joked. "Don't be cringe, all right?"

Chapter 2

"DAD, PLEASE," RACHEL WHINED. "YOU'RE embarrassing me."

Tate didn't seem to care. Chase watched as he continued to squeeze his daughter so tightly that the poles attached to her wrists splayed awkwardly out to her sides. Rachel grimaced and tried to push her father away, but while she had added a little meat to her bones, she was far from a large woman.

Woman…

It was hard to believe that this was the same girl who used to be frail and wheelchair-bound, the same girl who woke up every night shrieking.

Awkward gait and aids aside, Rachel had developed into a pretty young woman.

"Anytime," she heard Tate whisper, "Anytime you want to call me, if you're having trouble sleeping or if—"

"I know," Rachel said. She rolled her eyes in Georgina's direction, but despite this, she gave her dad an appreciative squeeze.

It wasn't easy raising a child on your own—Chase knew this firsthand. There were undeniable differences between what Georgina and Rachel had been through, but there were countless similarities, as well. Most important of which included that they'd both suffered great tragedies and their mothers were out of the picture.

It made Chase's and Tate's relationship a near-perfect match. A supporting, well-adjusted mother figure and a transparent, self-aware father figure.

Yeah, right. They made a good team like gasoline and newspaper.

At long last, Tate let his daughter go and stepped back.

They were standing in Rachel's dorm room, which was small, with two beds on opposing walls, a desk for each of the inhabitants, and matching dressers.

Apparently, Rachel's roommate wasn't slated to arrive until the evening. Chase counted this as a blessing. Her absence would give Rachel time to adapt to new surroundings and settle in before the chaos of orientation week began.

"Auntie Chase," Rachel said softly, her eyes downcast.

Chase was still getting used to this whole Auntie Chase business. Sure, she'd heard these words from Georgina for years now, but coming from Rachel? It was strange, foreign.

But she didn't hate it.

Chase stepped forward and hugged Rachel, a much more abbreviated version of the one that her father had given her, but she whispered similar words.

"Call me."

Chase had no intention of replacing Robin Abernathy, but while the woman was still in prison and the blended family lived together, she often acted as a sounding board for Rachel. There were just some things that a young woman felt more comfortable discussing with another female than their father.

The world had changed—preferred pronouns, gender fluidity, and inclusivity are the zeitgeist of our time—but some things remain the same.

"I will," Rachel promised.

Georgina walked over to the bed that Rachel had claimed and bounced her butt up and down on it, grinning the entire time.

Chase didn't like that look.

Fifteen… Georgina Adams was fifteen years old.

It was unbelievable.

And even though Georgina was slated to start high school in a week, it wouldn't be long before it was her turn to be shipped off to college.

Chase shuddered at the idea.

"Georgina, we should get going," Chase said.

The smile slipped off Georgina's face. Initially, Chase interpreted this as her niece realizing that the friend, she'd shared the same room with for more than four years was finally being set free.

But there was something devious in those green eyes, hinting at a much larger scheme.

"Georgina?" It was Chase who said her name, but the girl turned to Tate.

"I think I'm going to stay."

"What do you mean?" Chase asked. She felt her forehead crinkle.

"Just for a few hours, help Rachel get settled. That okay?" Georgina's eyes remained on Tate as she spoke.

"Fine by me," Tate replied with a shrug.

"I think Rachel will be okay on her own."

"Please?" Georgina begged. "Just for a few hours, then I'll take the bus back."

Chase started to shake her head, but Tate stopped her by placing a hand on her shoulder.

Something's going on here, she thought.

And she didn't like being on the outside.

"I think—"

"Come on, Chase, let's go grab some lunch," Tate said, cutting her off midsentence. "Let them hang out."

"But don't you—"

Now it was Georgina's turn to interrupt.

"Please? I'll take the bus. It's not a big deal, Auntie Chase."

"I could use some help finding my way around campus. I mean, G's gonna come to Virginia Tech in a few years, too," Rachel added. "It will be good for her to see the place."

Yeah, Chase thought, *there is definitely something going on here. These three can't even decide what to order for dinner and yet they're all in agreement on* this?

"Let's go have lunch and if Georgina needs a pickup later, we can swing by and grab her," Tate said, and then he lowered his voice and added, "It's safe here."

Nothing could be further from the truth. Every moment that Georgina was out of her sight wasn't safe, and Virginia Tech did have a history to consider.

But Chase had learned to keep some of the anxiety she felt in Georgina's absence at bay. It was easy to do when she was working, as Chase tended to become so completely absorbed by a case that she often lost sight of everything else, but this was different.

Chase sighed and gave in.

She didn't want to be the one to ruin the girls' fun. Besides, it was still early, and it was orientation week. This would be the safest week of them all.

Probably.

"Okay," Chase said with some difficulty. "Okay, we'll pick you up in two hours, Georgina. Stick together."

They moved to the door, but Chase hovered. Tate urged her along.

Back in the car, she allowed her eyes to drift to the dormitory building full of young, horny VT freshmen.

One thing that Chase hadn't yet mastered was turning off the analytical portion of her brain. It often took a backseat to the irrational part that had been molded by electroshock therapy and heroin abuse, but it was still there. And it chose this moment to rear its ugly head.

Statistically, one in six women will be sexually assaulted during their lifetime. And given the fact that there were roughly 3000 females in Rachel's freshman class, that meant that over five hundred will, in the future, or have already been, abused.

"Chase, it'll be okay," Tate assured her.

No, it won't.

Chase bit her lip to prevent herself from saying these words out loud. That was something she'd been working on, too; not blurting out the first thing that came into her head.

"I sure hope so," she said.

Like everything in her life, this was still a work in progress.

***

"Can't we just go somewhere closer?" Chase asked as they pulled into the parking lot of a fancy French restaurant. It looked like a nice place, which wasn't really their vibe. Hell, at home, Georgina's favorite meal was still grilled cheese sandwiches. "Just in case?"

Tate put one elbow on the roof of his car and glanced at her over the hood.

"Just in case of what?"

Chase shot him a disapproving look.

"You know what," she said flatly.

"This is hard for me too, you know," he said, lowering his eyes. "But you have to let go. At least a little."

Chase didn't agree. She'd let go of Felix and he'd been kidnapped by a deranged madman.

Things had since improved with her son to the point where their relationship had gone from copacetic to something close to a friendship. Not yet a mother-son relationship, Chase suspected that that ship had sailed, never to return, but she was grateful for what she had. There had been a time when she'd conceded that they might never speak again.

"Come on, let's just enjoy our lunch."

"Fine," she relented.

The restaurant was mostly empty, and yet the good-looking young waiter, maybe a college student in his own right or a recent graduate with a liberal arts degree focusing on climate change, led them to a table at the very back.

Tate pulled Chase's chair out for her, and she sat. The waiter returned immediately with a bottle of sparkling wine nestled in a bucket of ice and two champagne flutes. And then he offered Tate a knowing nod before leaving again.

"Tate?" Chase said, radar pinging in the back of her head. "What's going on?"

"Nothing," Tate said, but he was unable to keep a grin from forming on his lips. "Just a casual lunch."

Chase picked up the bottle.

She'd been wrong—it wasn't sparkling wine but champagne. The good stuff, too.

"Just a regular lunch with champagne?"

Tate, still smiling, shrugged.

"Celebrating Rachel going off to college, is all."

But that wasn't all, Chase knew.

Over the past few years, and at her behest, Tate had started taking better care of himself, becoming more concerned with what he was putting in his body and what he was doing with the outside.

And it had served him well.

It's not as if Tate had ever been a bad-looking man, but as he'd aged, he'd grown into his looks, which was rare for someone who was approaching fifty.

Their attraction ran deeper than just the physical. They shared an emotional bond and because they'd been through so much together, it felt as if they'd known each other forever.

Chase recalled the look that had been exchanged between Tate and his daughter back in the dorm room.

"Tate," she warned, "You know how I hate surprises."

Tate poured the champagne but didn't sip it yet. Chase twirled the glass in her hand.

"You don't know what day it is, do you?" he asked, ignoring her comment.

"I…" she let her sentence trail off. *What day?* "Tuesday?"

"Very funny. It's actually Monday. Try again."

Chase racked her brain.

Eventually, she gave up and Tate looked skyward.

"I'm not surprised that you'd forget. After all, it's been four years, Chase."

Even with this tip, Chase couldn't, for the life of her, figure out what they were celebrating.

"Sorry."

"You *seriously* don't remember?"

Chase shook her head—she was beginning to become annoyed at the inquisition.

"I proposed to you four years ago, three days after that, you said yes. This is the anniversary of you saying yes."

Chase cringed.

"Shit, my bad—I forgot. Has it really been that long?"

"Yeah, it's been *that* long. Are we ever going to get married?"

Chase hadn't even thought about it.

With the CVU growing, their reputation often preceded them since bringing down the Duffy Group, which included the Director of the FBI and the ATF Chief of Staff, they had more work than they could handle. That, in combination with raising two teenagers while maintaining a relationship with her tween son, meant that marriage was the last thing on her mind.

"One day," she said, not because she meant it, but because she thought this was what Tate wanted to hear.

And, as usual, Tate caught on to her lie immediately.

"You know, if you didn't want to get married, you could have just —"

"No," Chase said sharply. "I do. It's just that with the—"

She was interrupted by the sound of Tate's phone, which he'd placed face down on the table, ringing.

Chase watched as her partner picked the device up, looked at the screen, then frowned.

Sometimes, Chase wished that these things had never been invented. They were a classic, double-edged sword. Sure, they offered safety, a way to call someone if you were in danger. But they could also be hacked and used to trace your movements, both digitally and in the real world.

Plus one, minus one.

Chase suspected that the balance of benefits and drawbacks provided by these compact devices likely amounted to a net zero.

"It's Stitts," he said, and then answered and put the phone to his ear.

Chase watched her partner's face closely and saw his eyes darken as interim Quantico Director Jeremy Stitts spoke to him on the other end of the line.

"Yes, of course." A pause. "Give us time, we'll be there."

Tate's expression changed—he was in full professional mode now. When they were together, he left his chameleon skin behind. He showed Chase the real Tate. But when it came to work, the man was all business, which was something that Chase was both attracted to and also respected.

"What was that all about?" she asked.

Tate reached out, grabbed his champagne flute, and down the golden liquid one gulp.

"Our conversation about a wedding date will have to wait," he said. Chase raised an eyebrow, and Tate clarified. "That was our new case, Chase. And we're definitely gonna want to take this one."

Chapter 3

"I'M SORRY FOR CUTTING YOUR lunch short," Interim Director Jeremy Stitts' said, offering a conciliatory nod in Tate's direction.

Jesus, did Tate tell everyone about this lunch?

"No problem," Tate replied, although his tone clearly conveyed his displeasure at the interruption.

Chase didn't understand why getting married meant so much to her partner. They were already common law and they'd even bought a house to live in together as a blended family. What difference did it make if they didn't get all dressed up and say those cheesy words in front of a crowd?

Chase had a habit of twirling the engagement ring that Tate had given her whenever she was uncomfortable. She tried to do this now, but she'd forgotten that she'd taken her ring off and left it in the car—she always removed it while at work.

The skin on her finger where it usually was, was lighter than the surrounding area. Chase observed this for a moment then raised her gaze.

There were four people in the conference room—Jeremy Stitts at the head, Tate and Chase off to one side, and Linus Bowen on the other. A large TV hung on the wall behind Stitts and on the screen, connected via a live video feed, was FBI Director Hampton, who had been promoted following Joel Delvecchio's incarceration and subsequent, and very mysterious, death while behind bars.

But it was the man who took the spot at Quantico that Hampton had vacated, at least for the foreseeable future, that drew Chase's attention. After all these years, Jeremy Stitts' appearance remained unchanged. His hair was still perfect, his face unlined. His cane, a sturdy-looking oak number which he needed to walk thanks to a bullet he'd taken while working with Chase, rested against the side of his chair.

Linus Bowen, on the other hand, had changed significantly. He had matured, his jet-black hair, which she suspected he dyed regularly, was no longer styled like that of an 80's punk rocker. Now, it was tapered on the sides and the length on top was slicked back, accentuating his widow's peak. He was like a kid who had gone through puberty and was just coming out of the awkward stage.

Hampton had upgraded his glasses, going from the circular ones that reminded Chase of Dr. Matteo's, to something a bit more classic, with a straight top bar and subtle curve supporting the lenses at the bottom.

On the table in front of each of them were several folders, all closed.

Over the phone, Stitts had revealed little of what the case actually involved. But the fact that Director Hampton had been called in to consult from the Washington office suggested that this wasn't just your run-of-the-mill crime involving minors—if such a thing existed.

"I'm going to let Director Hampton take the lead here, seeing as it came across his desk first," Stitts informed them.

All eyes were on Dr. Hampton as he cleared his throat, and in his typical deadpan demeanor, he said, "Thank you, Stitts. Go ahead and open the folders in front of you." They all did as they were asked, and Hampton continued speaking. "A man was driving down a rural mountain road just inside the Wyoming border near Montana when he came across an 18-wheeler parked haphazardly on the dirt shoulder."

The first photograph that Chase saw was of said truck, taken from a side angle. It was old and in rough shape. The underside was rusted, and the siding, which had once been white, had long since yellowed. The dual back doors hung open, but the angle didn't offer a glimpse of what was inside.

"The man immediately reported it and if you turn to the next page, you'll see why."

Chase flipped to the following photo and inhaled sharply.

She'd witnessed some horrible crime scenes in her time, and this was right up there with the worst.

A boy lay on the ground, one hand outstretched, the clawed fingers buried up to the second knuckle in the dirt. Inside the truck, she counted at least five more bodies of other young kids, all males. Their faces were nearly identical: riddled with tiny rash-like bumps, chapped, peeling lips, skin that bordered on the color purple. Their dark hair was damp with sweat and plastered on their scalps. The only main differences were that some of the boys had dried blood beneath their noses while others had blood dripping from their ears. Or perhaps they all possessed both, and Chase simply couldn't discern everything in the photo.

One thing was undeniable: they were all dead.

"Jesus," she breathed.

"The driver is currently in quarantine, but we've cleared him as a suspect. Next page, please."

She heard Tate turn to the subsequent photograph, but Chase couldn't take her eyes off the kids and the interior of the truck. She spotted several empty bottles of water and a stained bucket, the purpose of which she could unfortunately guess.

"We believe this is the truck driver—he was discovered less than a hundred meters from the others face down in the dirt. Also, DOA."

Chase finally moved onto the next photo. She was instantly struck by the disturbing similarities between the children inside the truck and this man. They were different in stature, of course—the driver was hugely overweight, weighing at least 280 pounds, with thinning hair—but with his face turned to the side, Chase could see the same red bumps.

"According to the ID in his wallet, the man's name is Michael Lawson. Long-haul trucker with a checkered past. Everything from assault and battery to possession. Last conviction was for the small-scale distribution of meth in Montana. Spent two years behind bars."

"I'm sorry, did you say 'quarantine'?" Tate asked.

Hampton nodded.

"I did. As a safety precaution, the entire scene has been cordoned off. Local Wyoming PD and the Wyoming Department of Criminal Investigation are currently trying to get a microbiologist to come in to take some samples. Cause of death is, as of yet, undetermined."

"Did they invite us to take the case? Did Wyoming PD request FBI involvement?" Tate followed-up.

"They did not," Hampton said succinctly.

"But *you* want us to get involved?"

Chase's eyes went from the photo to her partner.

What do you mean, you *want us to be involved?* She wondered. *Six dead kids in the back of the truck and you aren't interested in the case?*

"*We* do," Stitts corrected. "The truck is registered in Montana and yet it was discovered just over the border in Wyoming. That, at the very least, constitutes transporting a minor over state lines. We don't need their permission or an invite. This is an FBI case—no, a CVU case, if I've ever seen one."

That was good enough for Chase. She was already getting to her feet when Tate signaled for her to sit back down.

"What? We should get going," Chase said.

"And we will. I just have a few more questions."

"Go ahead," both Stitts and Hampton said in unison.

"The truck—you said it was registered in Montana?"

Director Hampton was the one who answered.

"Yes. Michael Lawson is a freelance driver, but he's registered in Montana."

"Was this a company job?"

"So far as we can tell, it was not. Local PD reached out to Mr. Lawson's regular dispatchers, and they have no record of a job. But judging by the cargo, I doubt that this delivery was slated for a Wyoming Walmart."

"I'll look into it," Linus said matter-of-factly. "Dig a little deeper."

Chase noticed that Linus was still on the first photo.

She wasn't surprised by this.

Two years ago, when the CVU was overwhelmed with cases, they'd asked Linus for his help. It was supposed to be a temporary appointment, a month hiatus as Director of the Cybercrime Training Unit at Quantico, but it had quickly turned into a full-time gig.

And Chase was glad.

She liked Linus and respected the man's desire never to go out into the field again.

Given that the last incursion into the field had led to armed intruders breaking into his home, aiming for his office where he had taken refuge, his apprehension was understandable.

Chase's mind drifted away from Linus, and she focused on the bodies again.

"Who are they? Who are the kids?"

"That's the thing," Director Hampton said. "Nobody seems to know. According to law enforcement in Wyoming and

Montana, none of them match the descriptions of their open missing children's cases."

This time when she stood and slid all the photos into the folder, Tate made no move to stop her.

Montana, Chase thought. *We're going to Montana. Yee-haw.*

Chapter 4

CHASE KNEW INSTANTLY THAT SHE was going to get along with Agent Ralph Hogan from the Wyoming Division of Criminal Investigation. This was rare, as most of the time when the FBI was called in, there was at least a little push back from local or state law enforcement.

Ralph was in his mid-60s and looked every bit his age. His face was weathered, but his light gray eyes were clear and inviting. Thick, reddish eyebrows highlighted said eyes, and while thinner, the hair on top of his head was an identical shade. The man was a good twenty pounds overweight, and in a lot of ways, he reminded Chase of a version of who Tate used to be.

"Thanks for getting here so quickly," Ralph said after he'd introduced himself. This, too, was new; not just accepting of their aid but appreciative?

Had their plane passed through a wormhole and entered an alternate universe on the short flight from Virginia to Wyoming?

But the surprises didn't stop there.

Ralph addressed Tate and Chase equally. In her experience, members of law enforcement, specifically those who were brought up in a different era, would focus their attention on Tate and rely on him to introduce his partner, as if she were a trophy wife.

A trophy fiancé, as it were.

But not Ralph Hogan.

He had flagged down their rental car about a quarter mile from the crime scene, and they'd pulled over in front of a cavalcade of cars—some marked with Powell PD insignia, but most, including a series of large white vans, devoid of any branding at all.

Sandwiched between a series of small mountains, Chase could make out the outline of the truck she'd seen in the case photos in the distance, gleaming in the hot sun. Milling about the scene were several individuals, CSU members most likely, sporting full-coverage white hazmat suits.

Before takeoff, Chase had placed a call to Georgina, who had since arrived home safely from Virginia Tech. Her niece probed her about their lunch, but Chase glossed over these questions and broke the news.

"Louisa is going to be coming to stay with you for a while," Chase said.

"What do you mean?" Georgina had asked. "Is everything okay?"

"Everything's fine," Chase assured her. "Tate and I need to leave the state for a little while for a new case. I'll be gone a couple of days. Louisa and the boys offered to come stay with you while we're away."

Georgina groaned.

"What's wrong?"

"I don't need anybody to babysit me, Chase. I'm almost sixteen."

"You're fifteen and you're not staying alone in that house by yourself."

"Come on. The boys? They're so annoying. And they smell."

Chase had smiled at this.

"Be that as it may, they'll arrive before dinner." She could feel Georgina's frustration through the phone. "I'll be back before school starts."

"That's not until next week. I thought you said you'd only be gone a few days?"

"You know how these things go. Keep in touch. Love you."

"Love you, too."

Chase wiped the sweat from her brow with the back of her arm. She regretted wearing long sleeves, but she had no idea that it would be this hot in Wyoming. It was edging into fall, and being further north, she'd expected Wyoming to be cooler than Virginia.

She was wrong.

The sun, unencumbered by anything but a mountain range that anywhere else in the Midwest would have been considered nothing more than rolling hills, assaulted the barren earth.

Chase's mind went to the kids in the back of the truck. She hadn't noticed an AC unit in any of the photographs and the truck, like Ralph Hogan, had seen better years.

It must have been boiling in there.

Could the temperature explain their flushed faces, the spots dotting their cheeks and around their mouths?

"We're still working on cause of death. We brought in the state medical examiner and he's doing his best, but this isn't his area of expertise."

"I thought you reached out to a microbiologist?" Tate asked.

"We did, but we're still waiting for someone to show up," Ralph replied.

"Expertise or not, judging by the white suits, I'm guessing the ME suspects some sort of communicable disease?" Chase said.

Ralph sighed and she got the impression that the man was close to retirement and that he was more than eager to pass this case off to someone else.

This explained his unexpected welcoming behavior.

"It's just a precaution, but he's not ruling it out."

"Have you considered bringing in someone from the CDC?" Chase followed-up.

"Agent Trent Bain wants to hold off on that, for now."

Chase offered the man a curious look and Ralph clarified.

"Trent is with the Montana Bureau of Investigation. He's offered to help but when we heard about you guys coming in, he elected to stay on his side of the border."

"You don't mind if he crosses over?" Tate asked.

Ralph shrugged his heavy shoulders.

"Not at all. It's up to you guys."

Chase was once again struck with the idea that Ralph was eager to wash his hands of this whole thing.

"Considering that the truck originated in Montana," Tate said, "I think that Mr. Bain should be our primary touch point."

"Fine by me."

"Good. Make the call."

Ralph nodded as he pulled the radio off his belt and contacted dispatch. As he did this, Chase addressed Tate.

"Let's check out the scene."

Ralph told dispatch to hold on for a second and looked at both of them.

"There are extra suits in the van equipped with oxygen tanks and air filtration masks," he said, indicating one of the white vehicles parked to their right. "You're going to want to suit up before getting any closer."

The idea of dressing up in one of the marshmallow suits with the Plexiglass viewing screens made more sweat break out on Chase's already damp flesh.

It must be close to a hundred degrees outside. What was it like in one of those outfits? One-twenty? One-twenty-five?

Chase cocked her head as she considered this.

And how hot was it in the back of the metal truck, which acted like an oven, retaining heat?

One-forty?

Despite the sun beating down on her, Chase shivered.

Well, I'm about to find out.

Chapter 5

CHASE WAS WRONG; THE WHITE tarp outfits that they were forced to wear weren't just hot, they were absolutely nuclear. The second she put it on it became like a greenhouse and the plastic shield in front of her face was instantly streaked with her sweat.

"This is ridiculous," she heard Tate grumble. The man's voice was muffled twice before reaching her ears, once by his own suit and then again by hers. The worst part was that they still had to make it on foot a quarter of a mile to get to the crime scene.

See? I told you all that exercise would pay off.

Three years ago, Tate would have been out of breath by this walk without being further encumbered by the thick suit and accompanying oxygen tank.

Ralph had explained that Geiger counter readings had revealed no elevated levels of radioactive material relative to the surrounding area, suggesting that the threat, if there was one, was biological in nature. The Wyoming DCI Agent seemed relieved by this finding, but Chase wasn't comforted.

"Let's go," she said.

Together, Chase and Tate started toward the truck. With every step, the insides of their legs rubbed together and made a *swish, swish* sound reminiscent of the Katy Perry song of the same name.

And they were equally as annoying.

They were nearly there, soaked with sweat as if just having completed a half-marathon in Las Vegas at noon when what she assumed was a CSU tech approached.

Tate introduced them and then got right down to it.

"Does the truck have a transponder?" he inquired.

Chase knew that most long-haul trucks were equipped with these devices for insurance purposes and to track miles traveled. This would be especially true for an independent contractor like Michael Lawson, who would expect to be compensated for these miles. Except, that was for regular deliveries.

And this was anything but.

Therefore, she was unsurprised when the tech shook his head.

"We checked everywhere—no transponder."

"What about receipts in the cab, gas station stops, that sort of thing?"

"Unfortunately, no—nothing that we can trace back to any specific location, anyway."

Chase made a mental note to check with Ralph Hogan about Michael Lawson's credit card records. He might not be dumb enough to keep a receipt from a gas station in Montana where he made a pit stop, but he might have used plastic at a fast-food restaurant, and those receipts were often forgotten at the bottom of the greasy bag.

"Where does Michael Lawson live?" Tate asked.

Chase got the impression that her partner was stalling now. They knew the man's address—it had been listed on his driver's license that had been found with his body. She didn't blame her partner, though. No matter how many times you were exposed to the devastating violence that humans were capable of, it was still a jarring experience. And some people needed a moment to collect themselves.

"He lives in a suburb of Billings, Montana, with his wife, Susan."

Chase, who had been inspecting the earth for evidence, raised her eyes to Tate who returned the look.

"Has anybody informed the woman of her husband's death?" Tate asked, voicing the question that was on both of their minds.

"No, sir. At least, I don't think so. I'm with Wyoming CSU, though, so you will have to check with Billings PD or the MBI to be sure."

"Right," Tate said.

Chase changed the subject.

"Did you take samples of the dirt? From the tires? Might give us an indication of what route the truck took to end up here."

"We have, and we plan to send them out for analysis. The ME wants us to wait a few days, though, just in case they're contaminated."

Chase frowned but said nothing.

She was stalling too, she realized.

"You want to see the back?" the tech asked.

"Yes," she replied flatly.

"I have to warn you, however; it's not pretty."

This much, Chase already knew.

The tech led them down the length of the truck, and Chase observed numerous dents and rust patches on the metal siding.

Michael Lawson apparently didn't take care of his ride, which was uncommon among truckers. Their vehicle was their lifeblood and where they often spent more time than at home. They usually treated their truck the same way a rich asshole treated their coveted sports car.

"Ralph Hogan told us that the truck was discovered by a random passerby about six hours ago," Tate remarked.

"Yeah, that's right. A Mr...." The tech looked skyward as he attempted to remember the name. "Bo Kelly, I believe. He was traveling North to meet up with some family in Montana."

"Any idea how long the truck was here before Mr. Kelly happened upon it?"

"Can't say for sure."

Chase's eyes were drawn to the mountains.

"What kind of wildlife lives around here?" she asked.

"Lynx, coyotes, bears, you name it. Although, given the climate and lack of vegetation, there aren't too many out in the middle of the day."

"Sure, but given the scarce food supply around here, wouldn't the… *accident*… draw them out?"

The tech paused before saying, "You're right. But in this case? In this case, I'm not sure animals are interested in what we've found."

Before Chase could fully appreciate the gravity of this reply, they eclipsed the side of the truck and she found herself staring into the trailer.

And what Chase saw took what little breath she had left away.

Chapter 6

CHASE WASN'T SURE WHAT WAS more disturbing, the body on the ground—a young boy, maybe eleven years old, with his hand outstretched—or the bodies piled in the back of the truck.

There were six victims in total and even though she'd seen them all in the photos back in Quantico, it didn't do the scene justice—pictures never did.

All of their eyes were open, and their corneas were milky as if this was a defense mechanism to protect the children's minds from realizing the horrible fate that had befallen them.

There was blood caking their nostrils and ear canals, and their hair was greasy with sweat.

Chase's assumption about the purpose of the bucket, which she now saw was nearly overflowing with a dark liquid and buzzing with flies, had been correct.

Despite the mask and breathing tank, the stench that reached Chase's nose was awful. It curdled her stomach, and she was grateful that their special lunch had been disrupted before they could consume any food.

She had no desire to see escargot and oysters, or whatever Tate had planned for their meal, a second time.

"No maggots," the tech said, "meaning that the bodies have been here for less than twenty-four hours."

"What about the flies?" Tate asked, indicating the thick black insects circling the bucket.

"Didn't hatch here. Likely drawn to the smell."

Chase felt bile rise in her throat, but she swallowed it back down knowing that if she threw up, she would have to remove the mask. The tech had warned them that if they did vomit, they should hold their breath and get as far away from the scene as possible before disrobing.

Chase kept it together.

For now.

As Tate and the tech continued to converse, she moved closer to the body on the ground, dropping on her haunches to inspect it. In addition to the clouded corneas, she noticed numerous broken blood vessels in the boy's eyes. While petechial hemorrhaging was most common in strangulation victims, she noted no bruising around his throat or neck.

Chase leaned closer still, and then without thinking, she started to remove one of her gloves.

What did you see? What did you see in the back of that truck?

A hand suddenly came down on the shoulder and pulled her back.

"Not now," a muffled voice said. It was Tate.

Chase put the glove back on.

What the hell were you thinking?

Chase looked over her shoulder at Tate and was met with a stern expression that held no judgment.

He knew what she wanted to do.

Chase hastily got to her feet. Sweat dripped onto her mask but not being able to reach inside to wipe it away, she was forced to shake her head to clear her line of sight.

This served to also snap some sense into her.

She took a step back and surveyed the scene with a degree of disconnect. The truth was that Chase couldn't do much now that touching the bodies was out of the question. About a hundred meters from where she stood, she spotted another man in a suit hunched over a shadow on the ground.

"Is that the ME?" she asked. Her voice was hoarse.

"Yep, Dr. Mason."

"I'm going to go speak to him."

The more space she put between herself and the carnage in the back of the truck the lighter she felt.

The figure turned out to be Michael Lawson's body and the man in the suit turned to face Chase as she came near.

He was old and bald, with wide-set eyes and a bulbous nose.

"Dr. Bryce Mason, medical examiner."

"Agent Chase Adams, FBI, CVU division." Judging by the ME's reaction, or lack thereof, their reputation had yet to reach this part of the country. "Children's Victim Unit."

"Ah." Evidently satisfied, the ME gestured toward the body. "Michael Lawson, 52 years old. Similar injuries as the victims in the trailer: flushed face, coryza, maculopapular rash. Blood in nose and ears. There's also this." Dr. Mason pointed at an old-fashioned six-shooter lying in the dirt. Someone had marked it with a yellow evidence placard.

"Used?"

"Not for some time. I'm not even sure it works."

Chase nodded—she was more interested in the injuries to Michael's body than the fact that he had a gun with him when he wandered away from the truck.

This triggered an idea, and she glanced back the way she'd come. Chase had made clear footprints in the dusty ground, and it was easy to identify Dr. Mason's tracks, as well.

This wasn't the case with Michael. There were long streaks of disturbed dirt of varying lengths leading to his body, but these were frantic and less defined.

"Was he running? Running away from the truck?" she asked the ME, indicating the strange swashes of disturbed dirt.

"Looks that way. At least, at first. Then he staggered and fell."

"Huh." Chase locked this information away and returned her focus to the body. "I noticed petechial hemorrhaging in one of the other victims," she said. "Was Michael strangled?"

The ME shook his head.

"Damn it's hot in here," he muttered before addressing her. "The hyoid bone is still intact—I've ruled out strangulation as the manner of death."

"And the spots?"

"Cause unclear."

Chase knew that scientists and doctors alike were not in favor of guessing about pretty much anything, but she figured it was worth a shot.

"Any hypothesis on the cause of death?"

"I don't know for certain," Dr. Mason said predictably. "But based on the blood in their nose and ears, as well as the burst vessels in the victims' eyes, I'm leaning toward encephalitis and cranial hemorrhage."

"Encephalitis?" Chase was shocked by the man's words.

Dr. Mason misinterpreted her tone as not being familiar with the term, and he felt the need to explain.

"Swelling of the brain. Pressure increases and the skull, incapable of expanding, basically squeezes the gray matter until major vessels burst. I'll have to wait until I get the bodies back to the morgue to confirm."

Chase licked her lips and instantly regretted it. They were salty with sweat and made her stomach lurch a second time.

"What caused the swelling? The heat?"

It was nearing late afternoon, but the sun seemingly had no thoughts of setting anytime soon.

"There are signs of dehydration, as you can see here," Dr. Mason indicated the man's chapped lips. "But, no, I don't think that this degree of encephalitis was a result of the heat."

Chase scratched the back of her head and thought of Occam's Razor. But if all of the simple explanations were ruled out, what was left?

She'd been holding out hope that this was just all a horrible, tragic accident. Now, as much as Chase was loath to do so, she couldn't help considering the possibility of a biological contaminant.

With this in mind, she said, "What could cause something like this, then?"

"Again, once I get the bodies—" Dr. Mason stopped abruptly. "You know what? You're probably better off asking them."

Chase's eyes snapped up and she followed the man's white glove as he pointed in the distance. Two people approached, both wearing hazmat suits: a man and a woman, judging by their gait.

She knew instantly that the man was Trent Bain from the Montana Bureau of Investigation. Chase also knew that, unlike Ralph Hogan, she most definitely was not going to get along with him.

Chapter 7

"I'M TRENT BAIN WITH THE Montana Bureau of Investigation," the man said. He had a gravelly voice that didn't match his youthful face. Chase couldn't make out many of his features on account of the plastic mask, but she noticed a square jaw and dark hair that was short and brushed back. "Ralph Hogan with the Wyoming DCI invited me onto the case."

They had reconvened close to the truck and Tate quickly introduced them. Trent already knew Dr. Mason.

"This is Dr. Helen Niccolo," Trent went on, "she's a microbiologist and immunologist—CEO of Niccolo Pharma. Ralph said something about a potential biological contaminant?"

Dr. Niccolo was in her early 50s, with blonde hair and a pleasant albeit plain face. Her lips, which were on the thinner side, were pressed into a firm line. In one hand, she held a large black attaché case that reminded Chase of the one that housed her drone which was sitting in the trunk of their rental car.

"Dr. Niccolo, if you want, you can instruct us on how to collect the samples, and we can do it for you," Tate politely offered. "It's a pretty graphic scene."

Chase noticed that Tate had strategically positioned himself so that he blocked the view of the trailer.

"I'll be fine, thank you," the woman said.

"Dr. Niccolo has worked with us on numerous cases over the years," Trent said. Somehow, he was the one who was offended by Tate's words.

"Follow me," Dr. Mason instructed.

Chase and Tate parted to allow the two of them to pass. True to her word, Dr. Niccolo didn't seem fazed by the dead children and immediately set about opening her case. Inside, Chase saw a series of tubes and containers and familiar-looking buccal swabs.

"I'll also need blood samples," Dr. Niccolo told Trent Bain as she used the long cotton swabs to obtain cell samples from the corpse's noses and mouths.

"I've been advised to exercise caution with the samples in case—"

Dr. Niccolo cut the ME off.

"I know what I'm doing."

Dr. Mason put his hands up.

When Dr. Niccolo was finished, the ME led her over to Michael's body where she repeated this process.

"I'll draw blood when the corpses make it back to the morgue and ship them to you," Dr. Mason offered.

"Good," Trent said flatly.

"He's gonna be a problem," Tate whispered close to Chase's ear.

"Tell me something I don't know."

After about fifteen minutes of collecting samples, Dr. Niccolo indicated to Trent that she was done. They discussed something in hushed tones, and Trent nodded.

"We should back up until I have a better idea of what we're dealing with here."

Oh, so now she's being cautious?

Chase didn't like being ordered around, especially considering that she and Tate were the ones in charge. But Chase had already concluded that there was nothing more she could do here.

They all retreated to the row of white vans where Ralph Hogan waited.

"Ralph," Trent said with a curt nod.

"Trent."

"This is Dr. Niccolo."

"Nice to meet you."

Chase started to take off her sweaty hood and Trent glared at her. She glanced at Ralph, who was wearing jeans and a T-shirt and nothing else. Deeming that it must be safe at this distance, she continued what she was doing, and Tate followed suit.

It was like removing a garbage bag from your body after sitting in the sauna for an hour. Water dripped onto the ground where it was hungrily gulped up by the loose dirt.

Her entire shirt was soaked, and her hair was plastered to her forehead.

She caught Trent staring at her—likely because of the odd lack of pigmentation in her hair—and met his eyes until the mad looked away.

Dr. Niccolo made her feel more comfortable by pulling off her own hood. Halfway through, one of the clasps got hooked on a chain around her neck and Chase helped her get free.

Hanging from the necklace were two diamond studs.

"Thanks," the woman said, shaking out her blond hair. She grasped the diamonds in her hand.

Chase's initial evaluation of the woman held true. Dr. Niccolo had an unremarkable appearance, with ordinary features and hazel eyes that stood out against her bleach-blond hair. The necklace she wore seemed incongruous, suggesting a taste for the finer things, or at least a penchant for dressing up, indicating that the woman's exterior as a straightforward scientist might not tell her whole story.

This prompted Chase to reflect on her own life and how the work version of herself perfectly mirrored her home life. This was a sharp departure from Tate, who seamlessly shifted between various personas based on the situation and those around him.

How do they do that? Chase wondered. *How do they compartmentalize? How do they alter the personality depending on the situation or company?*

"Why don't we head back to Wyoming DCI? I've got a meeting room where—"

"I already have a command center set up just over the border," Trent interrupted Ralph.

Ralph deferred to Chase, and she looked to Tate.

"Sounds good," Tate said.

Trent removed his own suit and Chase saw that the MBI Agent wasn't as young as she'd first thought. There were deep lines around his nose and mouth that the plastic covering had hidden.

"Let's meet there in ten. You know where it is?" Trent asked Ralph.

"I do."

"Good." Trent waved a hand dismissively at Chase and Tate. "Give them the address."

Ralph nodded and Trent looked at Dr. Niccolo.

"I'll drop the samples off at the lab and get my team started analyzing them right away," the woman informed him. "Then I'll meet up with you at the MBI."

"That settles it then. I'll see you all there."

Trent wasn't in charge but he sure as hell liked to act like he was.

Yeah, we're not getting along, Chase thought glumly.

Chapter 8

COMMAND CENTER WAS A DRAMATIC overstatement. The room that Trent Bain led them to inside the bowels of the modern MBI building was nothing more than a glorified lunchroom. Hell, given the microwave tucked away in a corner, Chase thought it might be an actual lunchroom. A round table sat in the center of the room and it was surrounded by uncomfortable-looking chairs. A series of laptops, all closed, had been placed on the table.

Trent had wanted to meet up in ten minutes but Chase, who was annoyed at being bossed around and who had concluded that there wasn't much to discuss until Dr. Niccolo arrived, convinced Tate to check into a motel first.

They elected to stay in Wyoming.

Petty? Sure.

Now, nearly an hour after leaving the crime scene, everyone had assembled around the table—Ralph, Trent, Niccolo, and Chase and Tate. The only person missing was Dr. Mason.

"First up, the media," Trent said. "We need to decide how to approach this to avoid widespread panic."

Chase felt herself tense. This most definitely was not the first issue that needed to be discussed and the fact that Trent had brought it up was telling.

Tate sensed her apprehension and put the man in his place.

"No. What we need to do, is figure out where the kids came from."

Trent ran a hand through his short hair, aggressively rubbing it back and forth.

"Agreed, but until we clear the crime scene and—"

Trent's phone, an oversized space-age device, rang and he answered without hesitation or even a hint of an apology for the interruption.

"Dr. Mason, you're on speakerphone with Dr. Niccolo, myself, Ralph Hogan, and FBI agents..."

"Abernathy and Adams," Tate said.

Dr. Mason spoke up.

"I just wanted to let you know that we've created a special quarantine zone in the morgue. The bodies are *en route*. Should have more details on cause and manner of death in a few hours."

"What about the truck?" Chase asked.

Trent frowned, clearly not liking the fact that she was taking charge.

Well, you better get used to it, because I tend to do that a lot, Chase thought.

"The truck is still at the scene and will remain there until we finish setting up a warehouse where we can safely go over it. Not sure what we're going to find, though."

"The samples I took from the bodies are currently being analyzed," Dr. Niccolo informed the group. "Dr. Mason, prior to an autopsy, please draw some blood samples and have someone drive them over to Niccolo Pharma."

"Not a problem. We'll run some rudimentary tests in the morgue, as well."

"Good," Trent said, trying to regain control of the conversation. "As soon as you have anything, let us know."

They're wrong, Chase thought suddenly. The first step wasn't figuring out what they should say to the media or finding out where the kids came from. Their goal was much simpler than that.

"Dr. Mason," Chase said, raising her voice, "can you take fingerprints from the children and pump the results into AFIS?"

"I took fingerprints at the scene, and I've already passed them along to Mr. Bain and his team."

"I have a specialist at the FBI on hold. Send me everything you've got."

"Agent Adams, we have access to AFIS, just like you. I don't think—"

"What you think, Mr. Bain," Tate said sternly, locking eyes with the man, "is irrelevant. Dr. Mason, send the fingerprints to Agent Adams."

Trent glowered at Tate.

The awkward silence that followed was eventually broken by Dr. Mason.

"Of course, I'll get them right to you. Anything else?"

Chase pondered this for a moment then said, "I would also like a photograph of every item found on Michael Lawson's body. Every item in his wallet—his ID, everything."

"Will do," Dr. Mason said.

Trent, still fuming, hung up the phone.

Chase ignored the dick-measuring contest.

"Dr. Niccolo, Dr. Mason mentioned that he suspects the victims died from encephalitis. Any ideas of what the root cause might be?"

"I'm not a fan of speculating, but based on my observations, I can't rule out an infection. My deferential at this point include rubella, measles, erythema infectiosum, Epstein-Barr virus infection, pharyngeal conjunctival fever, dengue, or zika virus."

Dr. Niccolo may not like to hypothesize, but she'd come prepared—she was reading the list of infections from a prepared document she had in front of her.

Oh, that's it? Chase thought ruefully. *Pretty much every infectious agent in Grey's Anatomy.*

"Dengue?" Tate said. "I thought that was mostly found in India and Brazil."

"True—it's unlikely, but possible," Dr. Niccolo said apathetically.

As the rest of the group continued to discuss differentials, Chase's mind turned to the children themselves.

What a horrible last few hours they must have experienced. Covered in a mysterious rash, overwhelmed by the heat, dehydrated, likely hallucinating.

And scared.

Frightened beyond belief.

And then there was Michael Lawson. Did he contract the illness from the kids or was he the one who spread it to them?

"You're right, Agent Abernathy," Dr. Niccolo said. "Almost all the infections I mentioned have an incubation time of at least two to three days. Performing contact tracing on Mrs. Lawson is a good place to start."

"Has anyone reached out to her?" Chase asked, only half paying attention to what they were saying.

"Not yet," Trent replied.

"Then we should go see her."

"I have dispatched—"

"Call them back," Tate said. "Agent Adams and I will speak with Mrs. Lawson."

"Agent Abernathy, they're on their way. It'll take—"

"Mr. Bain, let me make this perfectly clear to you," Tate said, speaking slowly and deliberately. "Agent Adams and I are heading up this case. We appreciate your cooperation, but rest assured, we're the ones calling the shots."

The only person who hadn't spoken up yet was Ralph and he chose to do so now.

"The truck was on Wyoming soil, and we officially called the FBI in."

Chase appreciated the man's attempt to maintain the peace, but his comment wasn't necessary.

"Be that as it may, the truck came from Montana," Trent reminded them.

"No—the truck was *registered* in Montana," Chase corrected. "As of yet, we have no idea where it came from or where it was going. But it doesn't matter because this is a CVU case. Call your men, tell them to stand down—Tate and I will visit Michael Lawson's wife. In the meantime, it will be your job to figure out the names of the victims. We were told that none of them match the descriptions of missing persons from Wyoming or Montana?"

Trent Bain's lips twisted into a sneer.

"No, they don't," Trent said, and Ralph concurred.

So, it's gonna be like that then?

"Which brings us full circle to media involvement," she said. "Right now, it's best if we keep them out of the loop at least until we find out what the victims died of."

"The fastest way to identify the kids is to release a description of them to the public," Trent said stubbornly.

"Really? And what would that description consist of? Six children between the ages of… What? Eight and fourteen? All with dark hair and pustules all over their faces? Or maybe you want to release the crime scene pictures because those would in no way incite panic, right?"

"If this is a communicable disease," Trent shot back, "then we need to make sure that these kids haven't already spread it to their classmates, which, I think you'd agree, trumps the minor inconvenience of exposing people to 'disturbing images'."

"Our lab is informed of any spikes in infectious cases from local hospitals," Dr. Niccolo interjected. "Nothing has popped up or raised alarm."

"I still think bringing the media in and alerting the public is the play here," Trent said, clearly forgetting what Tate had just told him.

Yeah, Chase thought, *I bet you do. And with you standing at the pulpit, preaching to the masses, no doubt.*

"Noted," Tate said. "But for now, we don't talk to anyone. If there's any media leak, I know exactly who I'm coming to first."

Tate's threat was implicit, and Trent Bain wasn't the type of person who took this lightly. He folded his hands over his chest, lowered his eyes for a second, and then looked at both of them.

"If anybody else gets sick, it's on you."

"No, it's not on *us,*" Chase said quickly. "It's on whoever put those kids in the back of the truck."

She waited for a challenge that never came.

"Good. Now, Dr. Niccolo, I want you to head back to your lab and figure out what these kids died of. Mr. Hogan, we are assuming that these kids came from Montana, but they very well might be Wyoming natives. Go over every missing person's case from the last five years."

"And look for what? Young boys between the ages of eight and fourteen with pustules on their faces?" Trent said, using Chase's own words against her.

A scathing retort was on the tip of Chase's tongue, but Tate saved her from further muddying their already contentious relationship.

"I don't care what description you use internally. Just find out who the hell they are and where they came from."

Chapter 9

"WELL, THAT WAS INTERESTING," TATE said.

"That's one way of putting it," Chase replied, her eyes locked on her phone. Dr. Mason had sent her photographs of everything that had been on Michael's person. There were shots of his clothing, a T-shirt that was soaked through with sweat, dirty jeans, and a pair of tan-colored boots. Chase quickly scrolled through these banal items, before getting to the more interesting ones. The man's license, a Montana issue, revealed his birth date to be September 4, 1971. Other than the ID, his wallet, a cracked leather thing that looked at least a decade old, held only three other items: the first was a handful of bills and this struck Chase as odd. There were no health, no credit, or bank cards. The second to last item was a piece of paper. It had dark smudges on the corners, suggesting that someone with sweaty hands had handled it.

"What do you make of this?" she asked, briefly flashing her phone screen to Tate who was driving them toward the Lawson residence.

He shrugged.

"No idea."

On the paper, written in sloppy penmanship, was a series of twelve numbers, all six digits long, grouped in pairs and separated on different lines. At the bottom, there was a hand-drawn sketch of something that looked like a simple tree with a snake wrapped around the trunk. The doodle had been made with a slightly different shade of blue pen.

"A tree with a snake?"

Once again, Tate shrugged.

"No clue. Send it to Linus, get him to run an image search."

Chase nodded. That had been her plan all along, but she'd hoped that her partner had some insight.

The final item was a phone that looked about five years old. She didn't recognize the model, and the lock screen background was generic.

"A burner, you think?"

"Probably. Get Dr. Mason to ship it to Quantico," Tate suggested.

A text arrived with more pictures, these ones of fingerprints.

Chase forwarded everything to Linus, with an accompanying message to prioritize getting the fingerprints into AFIS. She considered her message, then added, 'as well as any other databases that you deem necessary'.

He'd know exactly what she meant.

Linus was an expert when it came to computers, and he was also an expert at gaining access to certain databases that were restricted, even to the FBI. He'd proven more than a little resourceful when they had been hunting down The Duffy Group.

Chase put her phone away and they continued in silence toward the address listed on Michael Lawson's driver's license.

Twenty minutes later they arrived.

"I think this is it?" Tate said with hesitation.

There was no driveway, just a patch of dead grass leading up to a trailer resting on cinder blocks. The building had white siding, the cheap plastic kind, that was covered in dirt and grime that had accumulated over the years.

Even though there was plenty of space to park on the lawn, Tate elected to stop their rental directly behind a weathered Volkswagen Jetta.

Neither of them got out of the car.

To Chase, the likelihood of Michael Lawson being an innocent bystander in all of this was next to zero. Any truck driver worth their salt would check what cargo they were taking, legal or not. And even if on the rare chance that he hasn't, or had been warned not to, Michael must've heard those kids in the back. Boiling to death, coughing and suffering from whatever communicable disease that had taken their lives.

And yet, both she and Tate remained in the car for several seconds. Breaking the news to a loved one, even if that person was someone as despicable as Michael Lawson, was not an easy task. You always had to be on guard, unsure of what reaction was forthcoming.

"You ready?" Tate asked.

"I'm ready."

They walked together up the mostly dirt lawn, and once again Chase was amazed at how bright the sun was despite the fact that it was nearing evening.

Why didn't I bring my sunglasses? she wondered. *Maybe because you were too preoccupied with the fancy lunch that Tate had taken you to.*

The trailer's screen door hung askew on its hinges and Chase peered through the woven metal.

The interior was a mess. Clothes were piled on the floor, a coffee table was covered with take-out containers, and what she could see of the kitchen revealed precarious stacks of dirty dishes.

"Who is it?" A harsh voice hollered in response to Tate's knock.

"Mrs. Lawson?"

"Who is it?"

A woman stepped out of the hallway and into plain view, cigarette in hand.

To say that Mrs. Lawson was rough around the edges would be like saying that this place was a palatial estate.

Michael Lawson might have been 52, but he'd either married a much older woman, or years of substance abuse made Susan Lawson look like she was approaching seventy. The woman's frame was stooped, and the nightgown she wore, which might once have been flannel but now was threadbare, hung off her thin frame. Greasy hair, chestnut at the ends but gray close to her scalp, hung in front of her face, which was devoid of makeup.

"Are you Susan Lawson?" Tate asked.

"I ain't askin' again—who the hell are you?"

Tate and Chase showed their badges and gave their names.

The woman scowled as she pulled on her cigarette. There was no offer for them to enter, which Chase probably would've declined given the state of the trailer's interior.

"What did Michael get himself up to this time? I got no money for bail. I done told him that."

"Mrs. Lawson, we're with the FBI," Tate reminded her. A dog barked somewhere in the distance. "I'm sorry, but we have some terrible news about your husband."

Chase watched the woman's face intently as Tate spoke, trying to pick up on any tells.

She got none.

"Michael's dead."

Chase expected some sort of response now, but the woman did nothing other than take another drag of her smoke.

"What happened?" she asked flatly.

"That's what we're trying to figure out. Is it alright if we ask you a few questions?"

No response, which Tate took as an affirmative.

"First, was your husband sick at all?"

"Was it a heart attack? Because all he did was eat shit while on the road."

"No, it wasn't a heart attack," Chase informed her. "But was your husband sick at all? Did he exhibit any flu-like symptoms recently or anything like that?"

Susan shook her head.

"No, Michael never got sick."

"And when's the last time you saw him?"

"Couple of days ago. He had a job that would keep him on the road for a week."

There was no compassion in her voice, no grief, nothing.

Chase had learned long ago not to read too much into people's reactions to bad news, as these could be as varied as the climate in Montana. And yet, this lack of a response was strange.

"Did he say anything about this job?"

"He don't say much about nothing. Michael's never been too good at talking."

"Did he mention who he was working for? Or what he was transporting?"

"Is you deaf? Michael didn't say nothing."

"So, you don't know who hired him?" Chase prodded.

"I said," the woman began, raising her voice a few octaves, "Michael don't—"

There was a loud ringing sound from behind her, a phone, and the woman cursed. She put her cigarette between her lips and walked over and grabbed her phone, a boxy cordless one, from amongst the refuse on the coffee table. Chase watched her go and then glanced at Tate.

He made a face.

"Hello?" The woman barked into the receiver. "What? Michael? That you?"

Chase's eyes widened.

"Mrs. Lawson?" she hollered.

The woman was too focused on the phone pressed to the side of her head to hear her.

"What do you mean? Michael, they're some cops here and—no, wait. Michael? *Michael?*"

Chase reached for the door with the intention of opening it and storming inside, but Tate grabbed her hand and shook his head.

The woman hung up the phone and aggressively walked over to them.

"Who the hell are you?" she demanded.

"Who was on the phone?" Chase shot back.

The woman's dark eyes fell on Chase and bore into her.

"That was my husband—that was Michael," she said flatly. "Now, are you gonna tell me who you really are and what the *fuck* you're really doing here? Or are you going to make me get my shotgun and ask you again?"

Chapter 10

"ARE YOU SURE IT WAS him?" Chase asked, trying to wrap her mind around what was happening.

"I know my husband's voice. It was Michael. Who the fuck are you?"

"Susan, we're with the FBI, you've seen our badges," Tate reassured her. "As for your husband, we found what we *thought* was his body just over the border in Wyoming—the man had your husband's license on him."

"Well, that must be fake, because it *wa'n't* my husband."

"What did the man on the phone say?" Chase asked, still unwilling to accept what Susan was telling them.

"What did *Michael* say? Nothin'."

"Mrs. Lawson," Tate began, "if that was your husband on the phone then we need to talk to him."

"I don't know where he is." The woman crossed her arms over her flat chest, her cigarette mysteriously missing.

"What did he say, Susan?" Chase demanded.

"Nothin'," the woman repeated, doubling down on her previous reply.

"I know this is confusing to you because it's confusing to us. We were convinced that your husband was dead and—" Tate paused when Chase pulled out her phone.

She knew how he would feel about what she was going to do next, so Chase had made a habit of begging for forgiveness rather than asking permission.

Despite what they'd said to Trent about not getting the media or public involved, they didn't have a choice. Besides, who was Susan going to tell?

The stray dog that wouldn't shut the fuck up?

"Mrs. Lawson, is this your husband?"

The woman leaned in close to Chase's phone, squinted, frowned, and then shook her head.

"I ain't never seen that man before. But he most definitely ain't Michael. What the fuck happened to his face? He got AIDS or somethin'?"

Chase put her phone away.

What the hell is going on here?

"That man was found with your husband's ID on him."

"Well, it ain't him, lady," Susan said, shaking her head dramatically.

Chase was at her wit's end.

"He was also found with six dead children in the back of his truck."

Finally, a reaction. No gasp, no, 'oh my', but a slight change in the cadence of the blinking of her red-rimmed eyes.

"Michael had nothin' to do with that. *Couldn'a*. It was him on the phone. Now, if you got any more questions, you gots to talk to my lawyer."

Tate frowned.

"Well, we're sorry for the interruption."

"Damn right."

The woman backed away and picked up her pack of cigarettes and lit one.

Tate directed Chase back to the car, and they sat in the vehicle, oddly reminiscent of how they'd been before walking up to the trailer.

"Tate? What the fuck is happening?"

"I have no idea."

Tate called Linus.

"Hey, *papa,* I got the stuff from Chase, running the fingerprints—"

"I need a trace on a phone number, and I need it quick."

"Landline or cell?" Linus said instantly.

"Landline. I don't know the number, but it's..." He told Linus Susan's address. "I need to know who called the phone less than five minutes ago."

"Give me two."

Linus hung up and Tate backed onto the road. He parked across the street with Susan Lawson watching them from the doorway.

While they waited for Linus to get back to them with the information they needed, Chase called Dr. Mason.

"Agent Adams, did you get the photos I—"

"Got them, thanks. Listen, I want to do one more fingerprint analysis. I need you to fingerprint Michael Lawson."

The man we thought *was Michael Lawson.*

"Any particular reason?"

"Well, I'm pretty sure it's not him. We just visited the man's wife and guess who called her while we were speaking to her?"

"Who?"

"Michael Lawson."

"I—I—" Dr. Mason cleared his throat. "I'll run his prints right away."

"Good."

Chase tapped the phone against her palm after she'd hung up.

"Any ideas why the corpse would have Michael's ID on him?" she asked absently.

"Best guess? Someone hired Michael to do the delivery, but he subcontracted it out."

Tate sounded confident, but Chase offered an alternative theory.

"What if someone didn't like Michael Lawson, and decided to lift his ID and plant it on the dead man?"

Tate scrunched his nose.

"You mean like they were in the truck with the... *uhh*... whoever the dead guy is?"

That wasn't what Chase meant, but the comment gave her pause.

Could it be possible that there was someone else in the truck? Was there another person with those pustules on their face and neck roaming the nearest town?

"Maybe," she conceded, although she figured this unlikely. The other car tracks at the scene had already been attributed to Bo Kelly, the man who had reported the truck. Could it be him?

Could he have planned this?

If so, why call it in?

The MBI might have cleared Bo Kelly, but did Chase really trust them to do a thorough job when all Trent could talk about was getting media face time?

"You have to hate Michael pretty bad to set him up for something like this. And it's not like he was being extorted," she said, eying the broken-down trailer. "I doubt he's got a mattress full of cash in there."

Susan Lawson caught her eye, and the woman flipped her the bird.

Chase shook her head.

"You heard Dr. Mason, Michael just got out of the clink for distributing meth. That business isn't known for generating long-standing and fulfilling relationships." Tate's phone rang. "Yeah?"

"Alright, I traced the call—came from a gas station in northern Montana, about a hundred and fifty miles from the Canadian border," Linus informed them. He followed this with the address.

"I need one more favor, Linus," Tate said.

"Shoot."

"Contact Canadian Border Control. Give them Michael Lawson's name and description. Advise them not to let him into Canada."

"Will do. I'll also call you when I have any results from the other stuff you gave me."

Tate was already on the road, leaving Susan and her shitty trailer in the dust.

"Tate?" Chase said.

"Yeah?"

"If Michael gets into Canada, we're never gonna find out where those kids came from."

"I know," Tate said and gunned it. "Trust me, I know."

Chapter 11

EVEN THOUGH TATE DROVE LIKE a man possessed, Trent Bain managed to beat them to the gas station/diner that Michael Lawson had called his wife from.

"I showed the waitress Michael's picture from his license, and she confirmed that he was here less than a half hour ago," Trent informed Tate and Chase. "He was driving a late-model Ford pick-up truck, heading north. I've got a roadblock set up just before the Canadian border, and his tag number is in the system. We'll get him."

Chase wasn't so sure.

"As soon as Susan mentioned that we were at his house, he hung up. Michael knows we're on to him. I wouldn't be surprised if he goes dark."

"This is a long-haul trucker we're talking about, not some criminal genius," Trent said.

"It doesn't take a genius to figure out that we're tapping his home phone," Chase shot back.

"Jesus," Trent grumbled. "What the hell happened?"

It was a rhetorical question if there ever was one, but Chase wasn't going to let the man get away with it.

"What *happened*? What *happened* is that I was told that the body found by the truck was Michael Lawson. It most definitely wasn't. That was what *happened*."

Chase's phone rang and, grateful for the interruption, she backed away from a sour-looking Trent as she answered.

"Dr. Mason?"

"I ran the prints from the body that we found at the scene, like you asked. It isn't Michael Lawson."

Thanks, doc, this would have come in mighty handy an hour ago, she thought, glaring at Trent.

"Do you have an ID?"

"Yes—the man's name is Bob Santilli. Ex-con, shared a cell with Michael Lawson during his last stint in County. A colorful character—like Michael, he's been in and out of prison since he was a teenager."

"Next of kin?"

"None that I could find. But I do have an address for him."

"Send it to me."

Chase hung up and when the text arrived, she punched the address into *Waze*. Bob Santilli's home was only a twenty-minute drive from the gas station, which made Chase wonder if perhaps Michael had made a pit stop at his ol' buddy's place before his mad dash for Canada.

She walked over to Tate and grabbed his arm.

"I've got an ID on the truck driver," she told her partner.

Trent leaned forward, eager to learn the man's name.

Chase left him hanging.

"C'mon, let's go."

It was a petty move but fuck him.

Trent Bain was an asshole.

Tate and Chase pulled away from the diner, leaving Trent standing in a cloud of exhaust a scowl firmly etched on his face.

***

The search warrant for Bob Santilli's house came through in record time. Lying next to the bodies of six dead children had a way of expediting things.

But while Michael Lawson's place had been dilapidated, Bob's was utterly condemned. He, too, lived in a trailer on cinder blocks but it didn't appear, or smell, like anyone had been there in months.

Tate tried the door, which was locked, but a sharp tug was all it took to split the rotted frame.

Guns drawn, they stepped inside.

"FBI—search warrant!" Chase shouted. The air was fetid, reeking of backed-up sewage. "FBI!"

Chase cleared the right side of the trailer, Tate the left.

Beer cans and plastic soda bottles covered the floor, forcing Chase to tread carefully as she made her way deeper into Bob's home. A flicker of movement drew her eye, and she whipped the gun in that direction, her finger slipping from the guard to the trigger.

"Don't move!"

Tate approached her from behind and put a hand on her left shoulder as he'd been trained to do to avoid confusion.

"FBI!" Chase repeated.

She crouched and took aim, and then relaxed when she saw a rat the size of a small cat emerge from a discarded pizza box.

They cleared the rest of the trailer and reconvened outside.

Chase was happy to finally breathe a lungful of clean air. The stench inside the trailer was God-awful.

"Call Trent," she told Tate. "Get him to have his crew go over every inch of this place. See if they can figure out who Bob contacted recently or if there's anything that might hint at who hired him."

"Oh, Trent's going to love that," Tate said sarcastically.

"I don't give a shit what Trent loves."

"I was kidding, Chase. I'll call him."

While Tate placed the call, she put her hands on her hips and surveyed their surroundings. The sun had finally decided to blink out and in its absence, a chill had formed in the air.

Chase shivered.

Earlier in the day, the temperature had reached the high nineties. Now, she would be surprised if it broached seventy.

Chase was unprepared for either of these two weather extremes.

"He's coming," Tate said, wrapping an arm on her shoulder and rubbing her gently to warm her up.

"We should probably be gone before he arrives."

"Back to the hotel?"

"Sure," Chase said, leaning against Tate's chest.

They both stared at the mountains for a good two minutes before either one of them moved.

Chapter 12

Back at the hotel, Chase set up a video conference call with Stitts and Linus. She wanted Hampton to join them as well, but the man was indisposed.

"I have good news and bad news," Linus said. "Which do you want to hear first?"

What Chase wanted was for the man to stop with these silly games and just share what he'd discovered.

But Tate, evidently, didn't mind playing along.

"The good news first."

"Right—I sent out multiple alerts to the Canadian border control, including several recent images I found online of Michael Lawson. He's still in the U.S."

That's *the good news? That can't be all.*

"What about the piece of paper we found on Michael's—I mean, Bob Santilli's body? The one with the numbers?" Chase asked.

"Still working on it."

"And the picture of the snake and the tree? Does it mean anything?"

"No, not as far as I can tell. Did a reverse image search, but only came up with a few shitty tattoos and they aren't really that close."

Chase frowned.

"What about the phone we found with Bob?"

"Burner—no way to trace incoming or outgoing calls. When it gets here, I'll take another crack at it, but I'm doubtful that anything will come of it."

"Great. And this was the *good* news?" Chase grumbled.

Linus twisted his mouth into a frown.

"What's the bad news?" Tate asked.

"The bad news is that I didn't get a single hit on any of the fingerprints from the victims. They're not in any database. And I mean, *any*."

Chase huffed.

They were getting nowhere.

"Chase and I were coming up with theories for how this all went down," Tate said. "We think that maybe Michael Lawson was hired to do the job, and he got spooked. Got his buddy Bob to do it for him, instead."

"You think that Michael knew what he—or Bob—was transporting?" Stitts asked.

Chase considered this. Both men had a criminal history but there was a major difference between trafficking meth and trafficking children.

"I'm not sure."

"But Bob had to know, right?" Linus said. "I mean, he had to hear *something*."

Again, Chase was on the fence.

"Probably. But what does it matter? They're all dead now."

"All but Michael," Linus remarked. "If he calls his wife again, we'll get him. If I got a trace on the landline."

"And if he doesn't?" Chase snapped a little more harshly than intended.

Linus opened his mouth but then closed it again without speaking.

Stitts relieved them of the awkward moment.

"I want to help build a profile, but nothing in Bob's or Michael's pasts suggests that they're anything more than middlemen here. And with no idea where the kids came from or where they were going…"

Tate leaned back and put his hands behind his head as Stitts trailed off.

"What kind of car did Bob Santilli drive?" he said absently.

"Lemme check," Linus replied.

While the man worked on his computer, Chase asked her partner, "What are you thinking?"

"Just that Bob had to drive to meet up and get the truck—I doubt he took the bus. So, where's his car? We find that, maybe we're closer to figuring out where the kids came from."

"Bob drives a 1999 Corolla, tag number 1ZB881. Montana plates," Linus informed them.

"I'll pass that onto Trent Bain, add it to the APB for Lawson's pickup," Tate said.

This pretty much wrapped things up, and they signed off.

Chase rubbed her eyes and looked at the clock. It was only 9 PM but given the time difference and what they'd seen today, it felt much later.

Tate read this in her face, and said, "You think it's too late to call the girls?"

"Georgina?" Chase scoffed. "She'll still be up. The girl's a night owl, you know that. As for Rachel, well, it's orientation week. She's probably at some kegger or a club."

Tate frowned. He wasn't as protective of his daughter as Chase was of her niece, but this rubbed him the wrong way.

"I'm sure it's fine to call them," Chase said quickly.

They opted for Rachel first and the girl answered on the first ring.

"Dad?" she had to yell over the sound of music in the background.

"How are you?" Tate asked.

"I'm awesome!" As Chase suspected, there was a slight slur to Rachel's words. "Just hanging out with a couple of friends I met. My roommate came, by the way. Her name is Dani and she's great. A history major just like me."

"Good to hear."

"What's that?"

"I said, good to hear," Tate repeated.

"What?"

Tate rolled his eyes.

"Never mind, just be safe, okay?"

"Okay, Dad, love you."

"Have fun," Chase said.

"Love you, too, Chase. Bye."

"Sounds like she's having a good time." There was the tiniest hint of disappointment in Tate's voice.

They were going to miss having her around.

"Yeah."

It took three rings for Georgina to pick up and when she did, the girl was whispering.

"What time is it?"

"Eleven—just wanted to check in," Chase said, matching the timbre of Georgina's voice.

"I was waiting up for your call—couldn't sleep without it," Georgina said sarcastically.

"Right. Louisa there with you?"

"She is but fell asleep about an hour ago. We were watching the new season of Love is Blind."

"Any good?"

"Not really. Kinda cringe."

Both of them went quiet.

"When you coming home, Chase?" Georgina asked at last.

"Not sure. I'll be gone for at least a couple of days. Call me if you need anything."

"Will do. Love you, Auntie Chase."

"Love you, too."

Having completed their parental duties, both Chase and Tate got ready for bed and slid beneath the covers together. Chase was still getting used to the idea of sleeping beside somebody. Even though she'd been living at Tate's place prior to their engagement, more often than not she awoke to him sitting in the chair.

But ever since Rachel's night terrors had all but vanished, Tate was sleeping more soundly.

Tonight was no exception, and within minutes Tate was snoring ever so softly.

Chase was a different story.

Every time she closed her eyes she saw the boy in the dirt, only he wasn't dead. He was alive, his swollen brain pressing against the inside of his skull, making his eyes bulge.

And he was reaching for her.

"Help me... help me..." the boy begged.

When her cell phone rang just before the break of dawn, Chase was the one still awake and not Tate.

Chapter 13

Trent Bain looked as if he'd gotten as much sleep as Chase had. There were dark circles beneath his eyes and his hair, short as it was, somehow managed to look messy.

"Patrol car noticed the vehicle about an hour ago, called it in," he said as Chase and Tate approached.

"And you're sure it's Bob Santilli's?" Tate asked.

"Same tag number, same make and model. I just got here so I haven't checked the VIN yet. But it's his. I spent the whole night tearing apart Bob's shithole of a trailer," Trent said sourly.

Chase ignored the man's ire. It seemed to be his default constitution, anyway.

"What the hell is it doing out here?"

They were pretty much smack dab in the middle of nowhere. The area wasn't quite as remote as the mountain pass where the truck had been spotted, but damn close.

The major difference was that Bob's car had been discovered in a lush, forested area, tucked between a small gap in the trees, and not on a desolate mountain pass.

Chase was impressed that anybody had passed by here let alone seen the car.

On the drive from the hotel, she'd noticed several farms, but that was basically it when it came to civilization.

Hands on her hips, she approached the Corolla and peered through the window.

Like his home, Bob's car was a pigsty. Empty burger wrappers rested on the dash and the center console was overflowing with soft drink cups. On the floor of the backseat were several fast-food bags, all covered in grease.

"Make sure CSU searches those bags," Chase said. "Might find a receipt."

She backed away, taking in her surroundings. Despite the circumstances, there was no denying that this part of Montana was beautiful. It reminded her a little of Upstate New York where her log cabin was located. After purchasing the house in Virginia with Tate, he suggested that she sell it. But their financial situation had improved considerably since Stu Barnes' cash infusion, and she really didn't need to let it go.

Chase told herself that it would be nice to vacation there in the summers, but they never did. The real reason she kept it was *just in case*.

Just in case things didn't work out with Tate.

"So, Bob parks his car here, and then hoofs it to grab the truck?" Trent suggested. The man was surprisingly more amenable in the morning, his previous comment about searching Bob's trailer notwithstanding.

Chase shook her head, pulling herself back into the present moment.

"Probably not," Tate said matter-of-factly. "Michael Lawson was supposed to be the driver, so I'm betting he picked up the truck and met Bob here."

Chase looked at the road. It was going to be impossible to discern the 18-wheeler's tracks from those made by a farm tractor.

"Then where was Michael's car?" she asked.

"Good question," Tate said. "I guess Michael could have stayed in the truck with Bob behind the wheel, and then he was dropped off wherever he parked his pick."

Chase sighed.

"Damn musical cars... but you know what? With all that maneuvering, I think it's safe to say that the 18-wheeler probably originated somewhere close to here." Chase thought back to the farms she'd seen. "Can we get a list of farm owners in the area?" she asked Trent.

"You think that some cattle farmer is responsible for kidnapping kids?" Trent said with a sneer. The man's agreeable demeanor disappeared as swiftly as it had emerged. "Kids that, apparently, nobody even notices are missing?"

Truthfully, this wouldn't even crack the top ten of the strangest things Chase has come across in her career.

"Lots of places to hide them," Tate said with a shrug.

"It's a waste of time," Trent protested.

"Mr. Bain, don't forget who—"

"These people are simple folk, people who just barely scrape by selling wheat and corn. I'm not going to harass them with this ridiculous theory."

"You're going to do what we ask you to do," Tate said sternly.

The Trent they knew and loved finally returned.

"This is bullshit. What's next? You want me to go through another man's absolute shithole of a trailer looking for *clues*? No—maybe you want me to go and bother one of the dozens of faith-based collectives here in northern Montana. Sip from their communal wine to see if I get a fucking rash."

"Mr. Bain—"

Chase cut her partner off.

"Faith-based collectives?" she asked. "What the hell is that?"

Trent pursed his lips.

"Spiritual foundations or institutes."

The reply confused Chase even further.

"You never struck me as particularly woke, Trent," Chase said. "I didn't peg you as a guy who sits down after a long day to sip on an ice-cold Bud Light."

Trent glowered at her, but she didn't back down.

"What are you talking about?" he demanded.

"What the hell are *you* talking about?" Chase snapped. "What is a faith-based foundation or whatever the hell you called it?"

"Cults, Chase," Tate informed her. "He's talking about cults."

"We don't say 'cults'," Trent said. "You big-city people come here and—"

"*Enough.*" Tate drew out the word. "New religious movements, faith-based collectives, spiritual institutions, cults, I don't give a shit what you call them. But you're right, we should check them out. Especially the larger ones."

Trent's eyes narrowed.

"I was joking."

"Well, I'm not," Tate said. "What are the biggest ones around here?"

At first, Chase was convinced that Trent wasn't going to answer. That suited her just fine—it would be more than enough of a reason to get this asshole completely removed from the case and Linus could do the research for them.

But Trent eventually replied.

"The two largest ones are the Path to Eden and Ascendants of Light."

Chase resisted the urge to roll her eyes. The names were so cheesy, so clichéd.

So predictable.

"Which one's closest?" she asked.

"Path to Eden. Maybe fifteen miles east."

Without another word, Chase retreated to their rental car. Tate had left the keys in the ignition, and she started it up. And then, just as she put it into drive, Tate ran over.

"You coming, or what?" she asked. "I need to get away from Trent before I strangle him."

***

Chase knew right away that the Path to Eden was the place they were looking for.

It wasn't the vibe, or the wooden guardrails blocking the entrance to a mile-long road, nor was it the massive compound she could see in the distance.

It was the name.

Above the barricade was a wooden sign with the arched words 'Path to Eden' engraved in it. Below the letters was a symbol: a snake wrapped around a leafless tree.

"You see that?" she said breathlessly.

"I see it."

Chase looked around, searching for a phone or some sort of outhouse or any other way to reach the people inside when Trent pulled up behind their car and got out.

"I know what you're doing, and it's not going to work."

For fuck's sake. This guy hands around like a bad cold.

Chase cringed at the insensitive thought.

"Trent, you need to—"

"There's no phone in there. The Path to Eden has shunned all technology. They do all their farming in-house and people rarely leave."

Chase wasn't surprised.

When are these people going to learn? Technology isn't bad, it's the people who use it that you have to worry about.

"Fine. We'll just walk up there and ask them if six of their children wandered off." As she spoke, Chase began to duck beneath the barricade.

Trent grabbed her arm and she glared at him.

He let go.

"We can't—it's a religious institution, an offshoot of the Latter-Day Saints. I don't know how you do things in the big city, but here in Montana, they're protected by law."

"So? I'm just going to ask them questions. Do you guys have a law against that?"

"I don't know if that's a good idea," Tate said.

"And why the hell not?" Chase was annoyed that her partner wasn't backing her up on this.

"There could be more kids. We go in there, start asking questions, they might get scared."

"The kids aren't from the Path to Eden," Trent protested.

They ignored him.

"Let's get a warrant then. Shut them down completely. I bet the judge who got us a warrant for Bob Santilli's house will do it."

Not waiting for an answer, Chase called Linus. He sounded wide awake, probably already hopped up on Adderall and caffeine.

"Chase, I was going to call you, but I wanted to wait to make sure you were up."

"I need you to reach out to the same judge you used for the warrant to Santilli's place."

"It's 6:37 in the morning here." Chase bit her tongue. "All right, I'll get it done. Shoot me the address."

"Don't have an address but the place is called Path to Eden—it's in northern Montana."

"Path to Eden?"

"Just do it, Linus."

"Okay."

Chase was about to hang up but then said, "What were you going to call me for?"

Linus' tone lifted.

"I think I found out what those numbers on the paper are."

"What?"

"GPS coordinates. Didn't recognize them at first because there were no periods."

"Really? Locations?"

"Yep. Let me ask you something: what do Little Learners, Juliette and Lea, and Tumbling Tots all have in common?"

Chase grunted. She hated Linus' games.

"I have no idea, Linus. Please, just tell me."

"They're daycare centers."

She was too tired for this.

"What are you talking about?"

"You're no fun. The GPS coordinates on that paper all point to daycare centers in major cities across the Midwest."

Chase's jaw fell open as she realized the implications of what Linus was telling her.

"You're serious?"

"As a rash—shit, sorry."

Chase didn't even pick up on the comment.

Bob Santilli, the man who was driving the truck, had a list of GPS coordinates that pointed toward deliveries at daycare centers. Before Chase could truly grasp the gravity of this finding, a Black Mercedes joined them at the Path to Eden's gates.

Dr. Niccolo got out, her hair immaculate, her mouth but a paper-thin line.

"Helen? What's going on?" Trent asked.

The woman was out of breath.

"I just talked to my people at the lab; they think they've identified the cause of the encephalitis." During the ensuing pause, Chase could only hear one thing: her heartbeat in her ears. "Measles."

For the second time that early morning, Chase was taken aback.

"*Measles*?" Tate repeated in shock and disbelief.

Typically, her partner was the ultimate chameleon, but his mask had slipped off.

"Yeah, measles," Dr. Niccolo confirmed. "But not just any run-of-the-mill variety. I think... I think someone has weaponized the measles virus."

PART II – Measles

Chapter 14

"**WELCOME, FELLOW GARDENERS.**" **ELIJAH KANE** gripped the sides of the pulpit with calloused hands as he addressed his people. He paused, then raised his eyes and stared out at the mass of parishioners below him. He was pleased that his congregation had swelled over the past few months. The last census had them at just over two hundred people, but Elijah wouldn't have been surprised if they eclipsed double that number now. "It is with my greatest pleasure that I welcome you all here today. And I'm ecstatic to see that our garden is growing. Remember, the seeds that we plant today will bear the fruit of the world we want our children to live in tomorrow."

His words were met with a series of claps and cheers from the audience. These continued until Elijah raised his hands out to his sides, indicating for them to fall silent.

"A special thanks goes out to all the new faces I see here today. And while the Path to Eden welcomes one and all with open arms, I would be remiss if I didn't remind you that there is no such thing as a free lunch. Everyone must do their part to help our garden grow. We work long hours at the Path to Eden, and without your participation, our crops will most definitely wilt. Our philosophy here is simple: we see technology as a burden. At first blush, you might think that a tractor or hydroponics are a blessing, that they help us become more efficient at our work. But this couldn't be further from the truth. God created us in his image, and this image did not include robots or machinery. God created Adam and Eve, a simple man and a woman, with no artificial intelligence, no computers, no iPads, and definitely no TikTok at their disposal. This is the true pandemic of the world we live in, not the coronavirus. It is these evils that we must fight against—and fight we must.

"We are a peaceful society at the Path to Eden, one based on love for both each other and for the land that God has graced us with. So, when we fight, we do so in the absence of violence. We do so by proving that we can exist—no, not just exist, but *thrive,* without what others abhorrently refer to as creature comforts. We want to prove to the world that we can live as we used to live, without machines and computers. And this is our ammunition in the war against the industrialized world. As such, the sole requirement to join us gardeners on this Path to Eden is to relinquish the hold that these evil devices have over us. You must willingly and enthusiastically give up all your electronics."

And donations are aaaaalways *appreciated,* he thought, but didn't say.

A massive uproar followed, and Elijah couldn't keep the smile from appearing on his lips. Nor did he want to. It felt good, it felt good that the message he had been preaching for nearly a decade was finally hitting its mark.

Poverty, wealth imbalance, disease, violence, and the lack of morals and guidance, could all be linked to the rise of technology.

It was time for this dynasty to succumb to the fate that befalls all dynasties—it was time for this one to come crumbling down.

That was the primary tenet of the Path to Eden.

Elijah took a deep breath and finally continued.

"If you don't believe you can't adhere to our principles, if there is any doubt that still lingers in your mind, you are free to leave and return once you have been cleansed. No one will stop you; no one will judge you for your decision. But if you decide to stay, know this: we support each other here at the Path to Eden—we are one large family the way God designed humans to live. You will find true love here, companionship, and fellowship. That is my promise to you. In return for your hard work and for spreading the message of the Path to Eden, you will be graciously rewarded in this world and the one beyond."

Elijah brought his hands together, closed his eyes, and bowed his head. "Now, we pray."

Everyone said the next few lines together and the smile on Elijah's face grew.

"Let the soil beneath our feet remind us of our origins and the path we must follow. To Eden, we return, to Eden, we belong."

When the customary moment of silence passed, Elijah opened his eyes and slapped his hands together.

"If you would like to continue your journey to Eden, you will find several individuals more than willing to set you up with complimentary housing and assign you your task. Thank you, gardeners." He crossed one hand and placed it on the left side of his chest. "From the bottom of my heart, thank you."

With that, Elijah left the stage and ducked behind a curtain. There he was met by his right-hand man, Derek Reddick.

"Excellent job out there today, Elijah," the man said. He wasn't smiling like Elijah, but this was nothing new. Derrick rarely smiled.

"Thank you," Elijah said. "I noticed at least forty new faces in the crowd."

Derek nodded.

"It was a great day for the Path. God has blessed us in return for all our hard work. We should consider increasing our food stores, especially as winter approaches.

"*Hmm*. Any update on the plot of land to the north?"

"It's owned by Tyson Foods, the chicken corporation."

Elijah's expression soured.

"I've never seen anybody there," he remarked.

"Not operational. I think that they're just holding onto the real estate."

"Then let's buy it from them."

Derek frowned.

"They have no desire to sell."

"Put some pressure on them. You still have your contact in the Department of Agriculture?"

"Monty Douglas? Yeah, he's still the Director, last time I checked."

"Well, let him know that we're looking to expand and that we plan to enrich the soil with our crops, while Tyson is doing nothing but ruining the earth."

Derek nodded and Elijah took a deep breath.

"Good. Now, I'm beat. You know what these sermons do to me, Derek. I need to retire to my quarters for a bit."

"Sounds good," Derek said with a stiff nod. "And, again, great job today."

"Thank you."

Elijah walked up the staircase to the loft above the stage. It was his favorite place in the entire compound—it gave him an impressive view of the church below, of the people still filtering out.

He stopped outside the wooden door and knocked twice. Then he opened it. Two smiling faces greeted him, both of which belonged to naked women lying on his bed.

"Hello Eve," he said, marveling at the big-breasted woman. "Hello, Mary," he said to the petite Asian counterpart.

And then Elijah dropped his robe to his floor and stepped forward.

Like the women, he was now completely nude.

Chapter 15

"**WHAT DO YOU MEAN BY** *weaponized*?" Trent Bain demanded.

The usual suspects had reassembled back at the Montana Bureau of Investigation, only this time they were joined by Dr. Mason.

"We isolated the virus from samples I took at the scene," Dr. Niccolo informed them, "and then we sequenced its RNA."

She picked up the iPad in front of her and flipped the screen around for them all to see. It showed a split screen of two different single RNA strands. The one on the left was labeled *Paramyxoviridae* virus, while the right was called *Paramyxoviridae*-modified. The modified version contained at least a half dozen extra base pairs. "Measles is caused by the *Paramyxoviridae* virus, which is composed of a single RNA strand. Basically, the virus infects your cells and then reprograms them for one sole purpose: to make more viral particles. These infected cells eventually burst and the virus spreads to others around it. The one you see on the left is what we typically find in children, although infections are rare amongst vaccinated populations. But this one? On the right? It's been modified. We're still doing more tests, but based on what we've already seen it do, it's a safe bet that somebody deliberately designed it to be more virulent and more deadly."

Chase was still processing the abbreviated immunology lesson when Tate spoke.

"During the Covid outbreak different strains naturally mutated—you sure this isn't the case here?"

Chase was impressed by her partner's question. Her own knowledge of viral infections was akin to that of a three-year-old's: lick germ, get sick, *cough, cough*.

"The thing is, RNA viruses *are* prone to mutation, but this change didn't happen naturally. You see, DNA contains four base pairs, adenine, guanine, cytosine, and thymine. But RNA viruses don't have thymine, they have uracil, instead. But this RNA virus has both thymine *and* uracil, a clear indication that someone made it in a lab."

Chase cursed under her breath. This, she had no problem understanding. Kids lick virus, get sick, get rash, brain swells.

They die a horrible death in the back of a truck.

"What about vaccination?" Tate continued with his line of questioning. "Were any of the victims vaccinated?"

Once again, Dr. Niccolo shook her head.

"The young victims were not vaccinated. We failed to identify IgG antibodies for the measles virus in their blood." She screwed up her face and added, "But, I'm fairly certain that Michael Lawson—"

"Bob Santelli," Trent corrected.

"Right. Bob Santelli was more than likely vaccinated against it."

"Are you saying that even if you're vaccinated against the measles virus, if you contract this strain, your brain is going to explode in your head?" Chase asked. She hadn't meant to come off as insensitive but trying to understand viral infection had momentarily deactivated the filter that usually intercepted thoughts from her brain before she verbalized them.

"And suffer from acute respiratory failure," Dr. Mason said, unperturbed by her callousness. "All of the victims died from a combination of encephalitis and respiratory failure, which, come to think of it, are rare complications from measles infection."

"Not that rare if every single one of them died from it, is it, doc?" Trent said with a scowl.

Dr. Mason just shrugged.

"The short answer? We don't know," Dr. Niccolo said, addressing Chase's question. "Without animal models depicting disease progression, we're simply guessing at how virulent and deadly this new strain is. There are cases of vaccinated people contracting the regular measles virus, however; people with weakened immune systems, that sort of thing."

Despite the woman's qualifications, her comments were sobering.

They were indeed dealing with a biological agent.

Chase further darkened the mood by bringing them all up to speed.

"My colleague at the FBI thinks that the numbers on the sheet of paper Dr. Mason found on Santilli's corpse are GPS coordinates for large daycare centers across the country."

"Holy shit," Trent said. "Someone's trying to use these kids to deliberately spread the virus. This was no accident."

For once, what the man said made sense. And it was exactly what both Tate and Chase were thinking but neither had the balls to utter out loud. But now that the ice had been broken, she rolled with it.

"On that same sheet of paper, there was a doodle of a snake wrapped around a tree. That, and the proximity of Bob Santilli's car to the compound, suggests that the kids all came from the Path to Eden cult." Chase said, ignoring Trent's scowl at the use of the word 'cult'. "We have to get in there, speak to whoever is in charge. If—"

"His name is Elijah Kane," Trent interrupted. "He's in his early 30s, good-looking, charismatic."

If the MBI Agent thought he was divulging the secrets of the universe with his remark, he was sadly mistaken. In Chase's experience with cults, she knew that all of their leaders were charismatic and could expertly command a crowd. They were masters at manipulation and their ability to convince the most susceptible of society, women, children, outcasts, incels, to believe whatever they were preaching came as second nature to them.

"But, like I told you before, Elijah is not behind this." Trent was adamant.

"Right, well, I bet my FBI profiler friend would disagree," Chase countered, thinking of Stitts. "I'm fairly certain he's going to tell me that the head of a cult is exactly the type of person we're looking for: an egomaniac with radical views, who wants to spread their message like a virus through the population."

Trent sighed and placed his elbows on the table.

"It's not him."

"How can you be—"

Tate cut Chase off.

"What's the philosophy of this Path to Eden faith-based collective? You mentioned something about shunning technology?"

Chase might lack tact but most of the time she could at least appreciate its utility, at least in principle. But it irked her that Tate insisted on calling this cult a faith-based collective. It made the cult sound more official, more respectable.

Tim and Brian Jalston had a cult whose goal was singular: indoctrinate young girls. Why was their 'philosophy' relevant? If you apply enough mental bandwidth, you can justify any action. Brian and Tim had themselves been kidnapped and were, surprisingly, given the opportunity at a better life than the one they previously had. As a result, they believed that it was their duty to save other young children from tough circumstances.

Sleeping with and wedding these women was just a necessary evil—but, hey, they were doing God's work, right? They got no pleasure from their harem of young women who performed whatever deed they were asked.

Right?

"The Path to Eden is an offshoot of the Latter-Day Saints, split about ten/fifteen years ago in the early two thousands. Their philosophy is essentially that man-made technology is at the root of society's issues. They shun it and live a simpler life, do everything in-house. Farming, campfires, that sort of thing," Dr. Mason offered with a shrug.

Chase was aghast.

"And how better to send us all back to the stone age than with a virus to cleanse the world? I don't know what your deal is, Trent, and I hate to break it to you, but this sounds *exactly* like something that this Path to Eden or whatever the hell it's called would do."

"They don't believe in technology," Dr. Niccolo countered, "and genetically engineering this virus requires some very specific equipment. And knowledge."

Chase's eyes flicked over the woman. Dr. Niccolo was just trying to be helpful, but her interruption was not appreciated.

"You think this is the first time that a leader of one of these cults acts or behaves counter to their 'beliefs' to get what they want? Have you forgotten about James Jones and the Peoples Temple? They started off as a socialist movement, but it became a full-fledged dictatorship, with Jones yielding so much power over his minions that they committed suicide for him. Or what about the Catholic Church? How many priests condemn homosexuality and pedophilia, and yet in their private lives—"

"Chase," Tate warned, trying to get her to slow down.

"No, it's true. We all know it is. You guys might be too woke to admit it, but all I care about is finding out what happened to these kids. And if your beliefs cloud your judgment, then maybe you should recuse yourself from the case."

Tate gave her *the look,* and Chase regretted the harshness of her tone—not enough to take her words back, however.

"I was just saying that a genetically engineered virus is counter to their beliefs, that's all," Dr. Niccolo said softly.

"And I'm telling you, Agent Adams, that Elijah had nothing to do with this," Trent repeated, leaning forward aggressively.

"You seem so sure of this, so absolutely certain… Trent, you wouldn't happen to be a member of this cult, would you?" Chase asked with unabashed vitriol.

Trent Bain held her gaze when he spoke next.

"I am not. But my half-brother is." Before he spoke the man's name, Chase had already what it was. "And his name is Elijah Kane."

Chapter 16

ELIJAH SIGHED, LEANED OVER, AND spanked Eve's ass.

Still naked, the woman blinked and rolled onto her hip.

"You ready to go another round?" she asked coquettishly.

"Time to go," he said simply.

Eve frowned. Mary started stirring now, too.

"What's wrong?"

"It's time for you two to go," Elijah repeated sternly.

When neither Mary nor Eve started to mobilize, he slapped Eve's ass again--harder this time.

She yelped and a red handprint immediately started to form on her pale skin.

"Go on, get the fuck out of here."

They finally started to move, scooping up their handmade outfits and stopped to put them on.

Elijah hopped out of bed and rushed to the door. He opened it and shoved the half-dressed women out.

"Elijah—" Mary protested.

"Go now, be one with God. Follow the Tath… downstairs. *Go.*"

Shaking his head, he slammed the door behind them.

Then he peered out the window and into the nave below. If anyone cared to glance up, they would have seen him in his full naked glory.

But they didn't.

They knew better.

The few people who had remained behind after his sermon to pray in the wooden pews kept their heads bowed.

An unexpected pang of sorrow came over Elijah.

I'm going to miss this, he thought.

He shook this feeling off and then roughly closed the blinds.

After a deep breath, he went to his bedside table and opened it. Pushing the sex paraphernalia and his journal aside, he dug into the bottom of the drawer.

The corners of his lips turned upward as he pulled out a cell phone.

He punched in his password and the phone unlocked. Then he scrolled to the only number in his contacts and clicked it.

It rang twice and then someone answered.

"Hello?"

"It's Elijah. Is everything in place?"

"Yes." The person hesitated. "Elijah, I just want you to be sure you understand the ramifications of what you're planning. The implications are widespread. Your flock reveres you now but after—"

"I know what I'm doing," Elijah said coldly. "I know *exactly* what I'm doing."

"Okay, then—yeah, everything's ready. When do you want to do this?"

Elijah looked around, his eyes eventually settling on his bed.

In addition to everything else, he was going to miss Eve and Mary. Of all the women of the Path he'd slept with, those two had been the best. They hadn't shied away from anything he'd proposed.

Yeah, I'm going to miss those two.

Elijah grunted.

But there would be others like them. Better, maybe.

There were always others.

"Soon," he said. Just as he hung up there was a knock on his door, startling him.

"Elijah?"

It was that nosy asshole, Derek.

"Give me a second."

Elijah scrambled to put the cell back in his drawer. He slammed it closed just as he heard Derek enter the room.

"Yeah? What's up?" Elijah said. If it had been anyone else, he would have shouted at them, asked them what the hell they thought they were doing coming in here without being invited.

But it wasn't just anybody.

It was Derek.

The man eyed Elijah's naked form suspiciously as he said, "The food stores are more than running low. They're almost depleted. And with all these new—"

Elijah reached for his robe and slipped it on. Then he put his arm around Derek's shoulders and guided him out of the room.

"I can deal with that now," he said.

But in his mind, he was thinking something completely different.

Elijah was thinking that if things went according to plan, they wouldn't need more land.

And they definitely wouldn't need additional food stores, either.

Chapter 17

"YOU HAVE TO RECUSE YOURSELF," Chase said simply. Her previous threat of this nature when referring to Trent and Tate's beliefs had only been made in jest. Now, she was deadly serious. "You have no other choice."

"I will not," Trent scoffed. "I see no conflict of interest here."

Chase's eyes swelled. She knew that she and Trent were destined to butt heads, but she hadn't pegged him as an absolute moron. A dickhead, no doubt, but not an idiot.

"Let me get this straight, your half-brother is the leader of a cult responsible for shipping children infected with a weaponized measles virus to daycares all across the country and you see… no conflict?"

"You're making a hell of a lot of assumptions there, Agent Adams," Trent said. "So far, all we know is that the man driving the truck parked his car in the vicinity of the Path to Eden. But what you fail to realize is that it's also fairly close to Ascendants of Light, which shares a similar philosophy, not to mention the countless other, smaller movements in the area."

"You guys love your cults with their names that sound like something out of Dungeons and Dragons, don't you?" Chase said under her breath. "Tell me something: do the Assholes of Light or the Perineum Sunners have a tree with a snake as their emblem?"

Trent's jaw worked.

"Let me see the drawing," he demanded.

Chase had no intention of handing over her phone, but Dr. Mason was more than ready to part with his.

Trent tilted his head as he stared at the image on the screen.

Then he shrugged.

"I just see a doodle."

Chase was incredulous.

"A doodle? Really?"

"It could be the symbol for the Path to Eden or it could just be a random squiggle. But that doesn't change anything. Nothing definitively links Bob Santilli or Michael Lawson to the Path. And until we can prove, without a shadow of a doubt, that the kids came from there, I'm staying on this case."

"If you don't want to recuse yourself, I'll have someone remove you," Chase threatened.

"Bob and Michael are not part of the Path."

"And how would you know that? Did your brother give you a master list of followers? Because if he did, I would love to see it."

"They're truck drivers—that goes against the teachings," Trent said. "Bob probably just drove past the Path to Eden and made a doodle of what he saw."

"Well, a weaponized virus goes against their teachings, too. But that didn't stop them from—"

"Let's just calm down," Tate, the voice of reason, cut in. "Trent, you can see that there is a *potential* conflict here. If we find out that someone from the Path to Eden is involved in this, their defense lawyer is going to jump on the fact that you were part of the investigation, given your connection to Elijah."

"*If* there's a link to the Path to Eden. Now, I don't know how you do things in Washington—"

"Quantico," Chase snapped.

"Whatever—but here, in Montana, we use an evidence-based approach. We don't work on assumptions."

"Really? The Path to Eden and the Assholes of Light use an evidence-based approach?" She pantomimed caveman-style arm movements. "*Argh,* cell phone evil. What is this? A shitty Stephen King book?"

Chase was in disbelief that she was actually getting push back from this man, an agent with the Montana Bureau of Investigation, no less.

Why the hell couldn't this cult be located in Wyoming? Tons of wackos there, too.

Chase would much rather deal with Ralph Hogan than this asshole.

"But you are correct," Trent finally conceded, his words directed at Tate, "if this does come to trial, there may be some… *complications*. I'll make you a deal: if we find a definitive link to the Path to Eden—and we're not talking about a shitty little doodle—I will recuse myself. But until then, I intend to honor the oath I made in the Montana Bureau of Investigation and the people of Montana."

Chase looked at Tate. Her partner knew exactly what she was gonna say.

You're in no position to make any deals, Trent. This is our case, and if we tell you're out, then you're fucking *out. If you don't like it, I'll go above everyone's head. I'll get Hampton to pull his weight.*

In the eyes of the public, the FBI's reputation had never quite recovered from ex-Director Joel Delvecchio's involvement in the Duffy Group, but, as he'd just reminded them, Trent wasn't the public. The FBI still held a hell of a lot of sway over other government agencies.

Chase took a deep breath and considered their options.

Maybe I'm looking at this the wrong way, she thought. *Maybe Trent's brother leading the cult is an asset, not a liability.*

"That work for you agent Adams?" Tate asked, giving her the final decision on this.

Chase continued to think.

If Trent was booted from the case, there was no guarantee that his replacement would be any better.

There were worse agents out there, people like Tanner Pratt who weren't just difficult, but who went out of their way to deliberately squander a case for spite and personal gain. And no matter how much of an asshole Trent was, she had to admit that he'd been at least marginally helpful to this point.

Who else could have combed through all of Bob Santilli's garbage in just one night?

"For now," she said at last. As soon as the words left her mouth and Chase saw a twitch of a smile form on Trent's face, she regretted her decision.

"All right, now that we have that settled," Trent said, further angering Chase by acting as if he was in charge, "let's get back to this virus. Dr. Niccolo, you said that it was weaponized to be more aggressive, right? What does that mean, exactly? Does it hang around on surfaces for days? Weeks? Do we need to call in the CDC?"

Dr. Niccolo made a face.

"My lab is still running tests. I think it's safe to assume that the incubation time has been reduced, but without knowing how long before contact and the first symptom appear, we're just throwing darts here."

"I checked in on Bo Kelly earlier," Dr. Mason offered. When this was met with blank stares, he clarified, "The man who first came across the truck? He's still symptom-free, which means that he's either not infected or that the incubation period before the virus becomes detectable in his blood is at least eighteen hours. And, like you, Dr. Niccolo, I also looked into recent reports from the local hospitals. Not a single record of a measles infection."

Finally, some good news.

"Susan Lawson mentioned that her husband never got sick. I'm not sure how trustworthy she is, but if what she's saying is true, then it's unlikely that Michael was coming down with something when he went to go pick up the truck," Tate said.

"In that case, I think this thing has an incredibly short incubation time," Dr. Niccolo suggested.

Chase was reminded of what Linus had said earlier.

You want the bad news or the good news?

She was wrong; they didn't have good news.

All they had was bad news and worse news.

As if able to read her mind, Tate said, "Maybe we stopped this virus before it could spread."

"Let's hope so," Chase muttered, and then she rose to her feet, collected her things, and left the room without another word.

Chapter 18

"NO DICE ON THE WARRANT, Chase."

Chase was in the process of bringing a piece of toast into her mouth when Linus spoke through the speaker of her cell phone. She never ended up eating the toast.

"What do you mean?"

"Just what I said. I put in the request as you asked, the judge said he needs more to go on."

"Linus, did you go through the same judge who granted a warrant for Bob Santelli's house? Did you tell him about the six dead kids?"

"Yes, to both," Linus responded, slightly exasperated. Chase had to remind herself that this wasn't a stranger she was speaking to or an asshole with the MBI, but a colleague and a friend.

She softened her tone.

"Did he give you a reason why?"

"Said that the circumstantial evidence provided wasn't sufficient for a warrant. And before you ask, yes, I sent him the picture of the tree and the snake, passed on everything you gave to him."

"It's just like Trent Bain warned." Unlike Chase, Tate hadn't stopped eating—he bit into a sausage. "It's because the Path to Eden is a religious organization. They're being super cautious."

"Fuck Trent Bain," Chase barked.

Tate raised an eyebrow and finally stopped chewing.

"Who's Trent Bain?" Linus asked.

"Some dick at the MBI. Linus, can you talk to Hampton? See if he can pull some strings?"

"This *is* Hampton's guy, the one he recommended," Linus informed them both.

"Still, see if he can do something about it. We need to get inside the compound. There could be more infected kids in there."

"I'll try. Anything else?"

"Yes, there is one more thing you can do: I want to know everything there is out there on the Path to Eden."

"I'll do what I can, but based on the fact that I found no records of that image anywhere online, I'm doubtful that they have much of a social media presence. But I can look into tax documents and that sort of thing. If it is a declared religious organization, they have minimum disclosure requirements."

"Whatever you can get," Chase said and then hung up.

She stared at her plate. She'd been hungry when they'd arrived at the diner but had since lost her appetite.

Chase pushed her plate away from her and sipped her coffee. It was only slightly better than the tar that Trent Bain served at the 'command center', which was saying something because she suspected that the man had poisoned her mug.

"I can't believe we can't get a warrant for this place."

"I can," Tate said, swallowing the last of his greasy sausages.

"Yeah, you seem to be buddy-buddy with Trent Bain."

"Not fair, Chase."

Chase rubbed her eyes.

"Sorry, just frustrated."

"I get it. But I've worked on cases involving these quote-unquote cults. Everyone is supersensitive about religious rights nowadays. And I know you don't like Trent Bain—I don't like him either—but we might need him."

"Why?"

"Besides the obvious, you mean? I asked some of my old colleagues about Trent before we came out here, and while the general consensus is that he's an asshole, he's also clean."

"Who'd you ask?" Chase scoffed. "His mother? Better yet, his half-brother?"

Tate gave her that stare again, the same one that had crossed his face earlier when he'd scolded her for not being fair.

This wasn't unexpected—Chase knew that she was acting unjustly. But she never claimed to be fair. Sometimes, ruffling feathers and upsetting people, her partner/fiancé included, was necessary.

Chase took a deep breath and massaged her eyelids again.

"What do we do, Tate?" she asked. "We have no warrant to enter the place, we can't find Michael Lawson, his wife is a cunt, and Bob Santelli is a dead-end. What we do have is a weaponized virus and six dead kids. Throw a cult into the mix and that's a recipe for a country-wide disaster."

Tate took a large gulp of his coffee. She couldn't tell by his expression if he enjoyed it or not.

"I noticed you brought your case with you."

"My case?" she said, raising an eyebrow.

"Yeah, your drone. What do you say we take a little time off? Explore the vast Montana countryside with your drone? And if we just happen to fly over the Path to Eden, well... there's no law against that, is there?"

Chase smiled. So did Tate.

Chapter 19

THERE ACTUALLY *WAS* A LAW in Montana that required all drones over half a pound in weight to be registered with the FAA, but this was just a minor detail.

Chase and Tate set up shop roughly the same distance that they'd found Bob Santilli's car from the entrance to the Path to Eden, only on the opposite side. They did a brief drive-by, noting that said car was gone, likely taken to the same quarantine area as the truck. They didn't notice anybody out and about, which surprised Chase. She thought that a proclaimed self-sustainable farming community would have people up at the crack of dawn, milking cows or gathering eggs from chickens.

Massaging rosebuds and reciting poetry to ladybugs.

It had been a while since Chase had used the drone, but it came as second nature to her.

Within minutes, she had the goggles over her eyes and the drone was in the air.

As usual, the vertigo that Chase experienced quickly subsided. She flew the drone higher than she normally would, wanting to make sure that if there were members of the Path to Eden milling outside, they wouldn't notice it in the sky. She didn't think they would; there was a reason why almost everything of interest was at eye level for humans—they rarely looked up.

Unless, of course, to thank or condemn a God that, if up there, didn't give a shit what his lowly minions were doing down on Earth.

If He did, then the word 'weaponized measles virus' simply wouldn't exist in any human language.

With Tate chewing on a blade of grass beside her, she navigated the drone over the arched entryway, then continued toward the compound. She followed a dirt road, open on both sides, that was nearly a mile long to the main building.

Still, she saw no one.

Frowning, Chase took plenty of photos of the compound to send to Linus later. Despite her distaste for cults in general, she had to give them credit: their buildings were often spectacular, and the Path to Eden was no exception.

The first building she encountered was the church, identifiable by its pointed steeple and windows made of colorful glass. It was constructed almost entirely of wood.

The pinnacle was the church; from there, the compound, which was roughly the size of a small city block, extended to the rear into a U-shaped structure.

Nestled between the buildings' two arms was farmland. She spotted everything from wheat to apples to corn.

Further still were other, smaller buildings. These were also made of wood and Chase counted at least forty of them. If she had to guess, she would peg these as the sleeping quarters.

There were also chicken coops and at least two buildings that were easily identifiable as livestock barns.

The entire compound was surrounded by tress, except at the back of the property. After a long stretch of empty fields, Chase encountered a very different building.

This one was made of corrugated metal and appeared abandoned. Chase zoomed the drone's camera in and snapped a photo of a weathered sign that read 'Tyson Foods.'

Everything she saw, Chase narrated to Tate.

"I think I've got it all," she told him. "I'm going to bring it back in. I—" Chase stopped. There, tucked behind the sleeping cabins, was a swing set and a home-made slide. "Shit, they've got kids."

"You see them?" Tate asked.

"No, but I see slides and swings."

As Chase lowered the drone to investigate further, she noticed a flurry of movement just within the camera's line of sight.

The church's front doors were open, and people were spilling out. *Lots* of people. More than 250 of them.

"Looks like the morning service is letting out," she remarked. "Damn, there are a lot of people here."

"Better bring the drone in before someone sees it."

Chase agreed and pressed the recall button on her remote.

The drone was programmed to return to the spot that it had taken off from, using both GPS and the camera to ensure that it landed in almost exactly the same location.

Chase removed her goggles, blinked several times, and stretched her jaw.

"It's huge," she said, unable to keep the awe she felt from creeping into her voice. "Did Trent mention how many members the Path to Eden has?"

The sound of the drone's four propellers grew louder as it came within view.

"I don't think so," Tate said after a moment of thought. "How many did you count?"

"Too many to count," Chase informed her partner. "But if I had to guess? Anywhere between two and—"

Chase was about to say three hundred, but a voice behind her startled so badly that she dropped the controller. She spun around, her hand going to the gun on her hip.

"Hi, there." The voice belonged to a woman in her mid-twenties, wearing what was obviously a handmade dress. In her arms was a bushel and inside the bushel lay a pile of wildflowers.

Chase relaxed.

"Hi," she said hesitantly, moving in front of the drone that was making its final descent.

"You know, if you want to meet Elijah and take a tour of the Path to Eden, all you have to do is ask." The woman smiled. "We are *very* welcoming."

Chapter 20

THE WOMAN IDENTIFIED HERSELF AS Lorraine Torkoski, a gardener. Chase debated lying about her own name and profession, but Tate offered this information readily.

Lorraine was clearly one of those hippie, of the earth people, as Chase suspected most if not all of the members of the Path to Eden were. If the woman was surprised or even impressed by the FBI, it didn't show on her face. She just continued to smile as they walked down the long road toward the church. Most parishioners had since cleared out, probably to wander off to perform their duties, but there were some that took notice. Tate chatted with Lorraine while Chase observed everything around them.

There appeared to be an equal mix of women to men, maybe 60/40 in favor of women. They all wore simple, imperfect, loose-fitting garments, designed for comfort and not much else.

"I admire what you're doing here," Tate said, falling quickly into a role that he believed would net the most information. "It's impressive, I have to admit. Now, I'm not against technology by any means, but some days, I'm sick of it, you know? The constant scrolling, the constant dopamine surges."

"You're not alone," the woman said in her sweet voice. "Everyone here once felt like you. Now, we've gone from living in a world that is artificial to something real. It's wonderful."

So wonderful that you guys decided to load a group of kids infected with the weaponized measles virus and send them to daycares around the country?

"How long have you lived here?" Tate asked. There was a lightness to her partner's voice that Chase was unfamiliar with.

"Six months." Lorraine looked down at the bushel of flowers in her basket. "Started off helping with the water filtration system, and then moved on to become a gardener. I love being a gardener. I love just being out here in the open, you know? Before I came to the Path, I was an IT specialist, believe it or not. Working on cybersecurity for one of these mega-corporations. But this is just more... *real*. I don't know how else to describe it."

"Did you come alone?" Chase tried to replicate the softness of Tate's voice but failed miserably.

They both had their particular sets of skills, and while Tate was a chameleon Chase could only be one thing: herself.

Take it or leave it.

Chase was going to be Chase.

"Yes."

"Do most people come alone?"

But being herself or not, Chase was vaguely familiar with the concept of diplomacy. She skirted around the question she actually wanted to ask. It was always better if the person you were speaking with, be it a suspect or victim or witness, volunteered information. It didn't guarantee the truth, but that was the most likely result.

"Some do, some don't. Some people come here with their significant other, others with a family member. Sometimes, entire families join up. Everybody is just sick and tired of the way that technology has negatively affected our lives."

This was the information that Chase wanted and she pounced.

"You must have a school then?"

"Of course," Lorraine said with a smile. "We are 100% sustainable here. Even in the winter when it gets bitterly cold, we don't need to rely on anyone else for our survival. That's the way God made us."

"How many children attend the school?" Chase couldn't help herself now and her directness proved to be a mistake—the woman's smile transitioned from pleasant to placating.

"I'm new here," she said with a prostrated sigh. "I don't have all the answers. But Elijah, he'll tell you anything you want to know."

I sincerely doubt that, Chase thought.

Rather than push the issue, she spent the rest of the walk planning what she was going to say when they finally met the revered Elijah Kane.

Suspicious that Elijah might be an asshole like his half-brother, she also planned the best way to put him in a headlock.

Lorraine took them to the front steps of the church and stopped.

"If you wouldn't mind waiting here, I'll get Elijah."

"Sure."

Lorraine darted inside the church, leaving Chase and Tate alone on the steps. The building was huge, but a far cry from the LDS and Mormon mega-churches that existed in the South.

Chase breathed deeply and took everything in.

There was a hint of a lumber smell in the air, which mingled pleasantly with the wind coming down from the mountains.

Truthfully, a technology-free world didn't strike her as the worst thing. For all the good technological advancements has done humankind, there was no denying its vices.

"Well, this day took a turn," Tate said out of the corner of his mouth.

Chase nodded.

"It certainly has."

"I think we should tread softly here," he warned. "I don't know if I buy all this peaceful living stuff."

"Tate, we have—"

"Six dead kids, I know," Tate said in a hushed voice. "But this isn't an official visit, and we have no warrant. If there are kids here, I don't want to put them in jeopardy."

Tate was right.

The Path to Eden might claim to be a utopian society, all wildflowers and roses, but if the kids in the truck really came from here, then they needed to be very careful about what they said.

Whoever had engineered this virus had no qualms about killing innocent children—the FBI's presence alone may incite another act of violence. And, unfortunately, cults didn't have the best track record when it came to preserving their members.

"Okay, I'll let you lead," Chase said.

Moments later, Lorraine returned, followed closely by a short man with silver hair that came to his shoulders. He had a young face but moved like a man who had spent years doing hard labor. Chase put him anywhere between thirty and fifty years of age, a considerable range.

This wasn't how she'd pictured Elijah Kane. She thought that the leader of the Path would be more like his half-brother, tall, dark, gait like a water buffalo. This man was wearing a pair of cotton drawstring pants and a loose-fitting white T-shirt both of which were frayed at the hem.

He seemed almost… *pedestrian.*

A far cry from Godly.

"Mr. Kane," Tate said, holding out his hand. The man looked at his outstretched arm and then shook his head. Tate didn't so much as falter as he retracted the gesture. "My name is—"

"I'm not Elijah Kane," the man said. His voice was slightly raspy, which again came as a surprise.

Chase expected Elijah to say something corny like, *we don't have individual names here, we are but an extension of Earth and God, and blah, blah, blah.*

But he didn't.

"I'm Derek Rennick."

Tate didn't skip a beat.

"Well, it's nice to meet you, Mr. Rennick. My name is Tate, and this is my partner, Chase. We're with the FBI."

Derek had no reaction to this.

"Lorraine mentioned that you would like to speak with Elijah?"

"If possible," Tate answered.

"Of course, it's possible. We're an open society here and we welcome all comers," Derek gestured toward the handful of people milling about outside the church. "Everyone has a job, and they must complete their job to keep things operating smoothly. But people are free to come and go as they please."

Then come I will, Chase thought.

With this, she expected for Derek to turn around and fetch Elijah Kane from whatever hedonistic ritual he was performing, but the man made no move toward the interior of the church.

"There is, however, one condition."

Of course, there is.

"Your cell phones and any other electronic devices on your person must be left behind before entering the church. Here at the Path to Eden, we believe that most of humanity's problems can be linked to technology. And carrying them inside would bring a dark cloud over our society."

"Not a problem," Tate said quickly, pulling his cell phone out and offering it to the man. Derek looked at Lorraine who gladly thrust the basket of flowers in their direction.

Oh, they're laying it on thick, Chase thought. *Not even willing to touch it, as if it might be infected with the plague. Or maybe contaminated with a weaponized version of the measles.*

Tate plopped his phone on top of the wildflowers. Shocker, they didn't immediately wilt and die. Chase reluctantly did the same with her phone, ensuring that it was locked first.

"Thank you for your understanding," Derek said, "I'll be right back." And then, leaving them again with the ever-smiling Lorraine Torkoski, Derek disappeared into the dark interior of the church.

Elijah Kane appeared moments later, and he was every bit the man Chase knew that the leader of the Path to Eden would be.

Chapter 21

"**WELCOME TO THE PATH TO** Eden," Elijah Kane said raising his hands out to his sides. "My name is Elijah Kane, and this is our garden."

Elijah was tall, muscular, in his mid-40s. He had piercing gray eyes, a square jaw, and short black hair. Unlike Derek Rennick, and most of the other parishioners that Chase had seen, Elijah was wearing a dark-colored robe that fell to his feet. He held out his hand and when Tate shook it, she noticed calluses on the man's palms. He offered her the same courtesy, but Chase declined.

"Sorry, kind of a germaphobe," she said, which garnered a sharp glance from Tate.

"Not a problem." Unlike Derek Rennick's gravelly voice, this man's words dripped with honey. "Derek tells me that you're with the FBI."

"That's correct," Tate replied. He refrained from offering the nature of their business, instead allowing Elijah to guess.

"Sick of the daily grind?"

Tate smirked.

"Something like that."

"Come with me, I'll show you around."

Tate and Chase followed, with Derek picking up the rear. Lorraine stayed behind with their cell phones.

"This here is our main congregation. We meet three times a day, morning, noon, and evening," Elijah announced with an element of pride.

Chase was expecting something grandiose but instead was met by a very simple interior. The pews, like the outside of the building, were all made of wood, and while there was a stage, it was only slightly elevated. Above that, was some sort of loft, fully enclosed, with curtains drawn over windows that looked out over the church.

"This isn't just a place to pray, but it plays an important role in building and maintaining our community. We believe in the value of face-to-face contact, rather than via digital means. Video calls don't allow for the nuances of human interaction."

This, Chase was apt to agree with.

"Over the past nine years, we have built a society of peaceful people who love each other and who live a totally and completely self-sustainable existence. One that doesn't condemn family values but reinforces them."

Elijah continued to lead them through the rows of pews and towards the stage. Once there, however, the man took a sharp left.

He opened a wooden door with a rudimentary metal latch and Chase was once again welcomed by the bright Montana sun.

She was forced to squint and use the blade of her hand to shield her eyes, as she'd done back at the crime scene.

"And this... is Eden," Elijah said, indicating a massive stretch of farmland that Chase from the drone.

Without the filter of the drone's camera, the garden appeared far more impressive and contained many more crops that Chase hadn't initially recognized.

There were raspberry bushes, carrots, leeks, green onions, potatoes, squash, and countless other vegetables.

"This is a lot of food—how many members do you currently have?" Tate asked.

"At last count, two-hundred and ninety," Elijah replied, pride once again creeping into his voice, "and, like our crops, we are growing every day. People are drawn to a simpler and yet more fulfilling life."

"Looks like you have everything you need here to keep everyone healthy and happy," Tate remarked. Chase wasn't sure if this was a passing comment or a leading question. Tate was so good at pretending that even she had a hard time recognizing what was real and fake with him.

"Thank you, that's what we strive for here at the Path to Eden. We can grow pretty much everything we need, and we get our water from an endless well. Whatever we aren't able to produce on our own, we utilize a series of trade networks with other similar-minded organizations nearby."

"What about medicine?" Chase blurted.

Elijah Kane's gray eyes met hers.

"Everything we need to heal ourselves comes from the earth and the sun."

The man was an expert speaker, charismatic, all the things that someone who led people and convinced them that his way of life was the right way, the *only* way, to live ought to be. But Chase thought she noticed a slight hesitation in his voice when he made this comment.

She committed this to memory.

Elijah took them down one of the hundreds of rows of crops. Several women, indistinguishable from Lorraine, tended to the fruits and vegetables.

"Nearly three-hundred people," Tate mused. "I understand that your values prohibit violence, but I would think that occasionally you get a bad egg?"

What are you getting at, Tate?

"We are a peaceful society here," Elijah said.

"Yeah, but with kids? You know how they can be," Chase added, gaging his reaction.

Something dark crossed over Elijah's eyes, and then vanished.

"Derek Lynn Cott was an unfortunate situation. He was a troubled young man, and there is no excuse for what he did. But as I suspect Lorraine told you already, people are free to come and go as they please. Dylan elected to leave and what happened to him after that, well, that was beyond our control."

Derek Lynn Cott? What is he talking about? Chase wondered.

"Of course," Tate said, playing along. "One bad egg doesn't spoil the whole bunch."

"That's right." The pious man nodded. "Would you like to see the sleeping quarters?"

I would like to get the hell out of this creepy place, Chase thought.

"Yes, that would be—"

Tate's approach was undoubtedly working, but Chase's patience had run out.

"We don't want to waste any more of your time, Elijah. The reason we're here is that we're looking for missing children," Chase lied.

Elijah frowned.

"Perhaps I should have clarified. Our doors are open to anyone… anyone of age, of course. We're not in the habit of accepting children without their parents' permission."

"What about the kids that grow up here? Any of those ever go missing?"

Elijah laughed.

"That is simply not possible. Even the young ones have jobs and if one person doesn't do their part, the entire system crumbles. We would notice if someone suddenly disappeared. A chain is only as strong as its weakest link."

Chase noticed that several of the women who were working the crops had taken notice of them. Most just went about their business as usual, but one in particular, a woman with dark hair and bushy eyebrows, seemed to be listening intently to their conversation.

"Is that what happened with Dylan? He didn't do his job?"

Elijah offered her a tired smile.

"That was unfortunate," he said simply. "Now, would you like to see the sleeping quarters? They're modest but comfortable.

Chase reached for Tate's arm, and he got the signal.

"Actually, we have a meeting we must attend. But I want to thank you for your hospitality. And, again, I'm very impressed by what you've done here."

Elijah didn't skip a beat.

"Oh no, it's not *my* doing. It's the work of the Lord and everyone here in this community."

And with that, they turned to leave, but before they did, Chase made sure to lock eyes with the woman with the dark hair.

Chapter 22

CHASE WAITED UNTIL THEY WERE back in the car before taking out her cell phone. She inspected the device for several minutes. Satisfied that it hadn't been tampered with, she called Linus.

"Hey, Chase, how's it going?"

"Fine." Chase recalled her previous conversation with the man and added, "Good." She stopped just short of asking Linus how he was doing. She'd never been one for small talk. "Any update on the warrant?"

"Not yet. I made your concerns known to Director Hampton, and he said he was on it."

"Thanks. Did you find out anything about the Path to Eden?"

"A little, but as I warned you, they don't have much of an online footprint. Doesn't jive with their philosophy, you know?"

Chase pictured the vast farmland and the busy hands. No, it surely didn't.

"All right, I'm going to put you on speaker. Tell us what you've got."

"Well, according to their tax filings, the Path to Eden has one-hundred and fifteen registered members. They report only paltry earnings, but you know how these things are. It's not a good look for the IRS to be digging into these supposed peace cults when Amazon doesn't pay a single dollar in taxes. *Aaaaanyway,* the man in charge is Elijah Kane, but you already knew that. Forty-two years old, born to Ellery and Edna Kane. Only child. Up until about ten years ago, the entire Kane clan were big supporters of the Latter-Day Saints—I have several tax receipts from surprisingly large donations. I also found an archived LinkedIn profile for Elijah. He did his undergrad at Montana State University and got a Master's in communication from the University of Montana."

This made sense. Even during the short period she had interacted with Elijah, his proficiency in conveying his thoughts and beliefs was unmistakable.

"You said he's an only child?" Tate asked.

"That is correct."

"Trent Bain claims that he is Elijah's half-brother," Chase said.

There was a short pause.

"Trent Bain? The guy from the MBI you're working with?"

"Yeah—can you check into that, Linus?" Chase asked.

"Will do."

Chase waited for a beat and ran the conversation she'd had with Elijah Kane back.

"I need everything you can find on Dylan Lynn Cott, too."

"That's all I have to go on? A name?"

"I bet he's got a criminal record. He's probably young. Maybe not even in his twenties yet."

"Okay, give me a second." Chase heard Linus start typing and muted their end of the call.

"What do you think? I asked that question about kids and Elijah got this look in his eyes."

"I saw it," Tate confirmed. "He was quick to bring up, Dylan."

"Maybe too quick. Could be that we caught him off guard and even though he was thinking about the kids in the truck, Elijah used this Dylan story to cover his emotions?"

Tate didn't bite.

"It's a stretch, Chase."

"What is your general opinion the man?" she asked.

"I mean, to be honest? He's precisely who I thought he would be."

"Yeah, my thoughts exactly."

"Okay, got it," Linus cut in, and Chase took the phone off mute. "Dylan was 14 years old when he was picked up by the authorities. He was charged with indecent exposure and molestation of a minor in the state of Montana. Spent 18 months in juvie. He was released at 16 on his own recognizance."

"Jesus," Tate cursed.

"Bad egg, my ass," Chase muttered. "More like a rotten fucking henhouse. You have a recent address on Dylan?"

"I have something here, an apartment complex in downtown Billings. This is more than a year old, though."

"Send it to my phone, could be worth a look."

"Done."

"Linus, one more thing," Chase said, recalling another strange reaction that Elijah had had to one of her questions. "Do a quick check on Elijah Kane's health records. I want to know if he or someone close to him suffers from any chronic illnesses."

"You picked up on that too?" Tate said and Chase nodded.

"Health records are notoriously hard to access—"

"We don't need to know exactly what the condition is, just if the man has an account at a CVS pharmacy in town," Tate said, following up on her line of inquiry.

"That, I can do. Take care."

Chase hung up.

"Where to now?" Tate asked.

Chase thought about this.

"Well, Elijah Kane professes that the Path to Eden is a utopia, and I bet everyone at the compound will just spew the party line. So, why don't we speak to the one kid who broke the mold?" she said. "Let's go find this Dylan Lynn Cott."

Chapter 23

THE LAST KNOWN ADDRESS FOR Dylan Lynn Cott was in a seedy part of Billings, Montana. Like almost every major city, Montana had its nice areas, and it's not-so-nice areas. And then there was the area that Dylan had listed as his address on the release form after getting out of juvie.

Chase didn't get her hopes up. People like Dylan Cott, people who molested and raped little girls, tended to move around a lot.

They tended to follow their prey.

And while Elijah had almost politely referred to the kid as a bad seed, Chase had a different opinion.

He was a predator.

Chase made sure that she kept her hand on the butt of her gun when Tate knocked on the apartment door of Dylan's last known address.

She didn't expect anybody to answer. After all, they'd spied several spotters outside, young kids just sitting on their bikes, pretending not to look at them, but most definitely taking note. The second they were out of view, Chase knew that these kids would call their older friends and brothers inside the apartment complex and let them know that 5-0 had arrived.

Chase didn't blame them. Unlike Dylan, these kids had little choice in their illegal activity. They had no fathers, no role models. Likely their mothers were either addicts or worked three jobs to support the family and even then, they couldn't make ends meet. It was hard to expect a young kid to turn down work offered by an uncle say or an older friend from the neighborhood. Especially when just moving a package from point A to point B could net them more cash than all of the income from their mothers' three jobs combined.

They started as spotters, were promoted to runners, and then, as Al Pacino in Scarface famously stated, the world was theirs.

But someone did answer the door.

"What do you want?" It was impossible to tell if the voice belonged to a man or woman.

"Were looking for Dylan Cott," Tate said.

"He ain't here."

"Any idea when he'll be back?" Chase asked hopefully. At least this androgynous person knew who Dylan Cott was. That was a start.

"He dead."

There goes that hope.

"We're from the FBI—can we ask you a few questions?" Chase said, acutely aware that this conversation was following the same pattern as the one with Susan Lawson.

And that one hadn't ended well.

"Whatever Dylan did, I don't want to hear it. He dead, he *gon'*. Why can't you just leave him alone?"

"We don't know what he did," Tate lied. They know exactly what Dylan had done to the nine-year-old girl. "What we want to know about is his time in the Path to Eden."

A deadbolt retraced and the door opened a few inches before the security chain caught.

Chase found herself staring into the bloodshot eye and dilated pupil of a woman who she would've bet every cent she'd ever come in contact with was addicted to meth.

It wasn't just the look, but the smell. The apartment reeked of burning plastic.

It took an addict to know an addict.

"You're from that *cult*, aren't you?"

"No, we're from the FBI." To prove his point, Tate flashed his badge.

The woman barely looked at it.

"Good. *Fuck* those guys."

"What can you tell us about Dylan's time there?"

"*Our* time there. Yeah, that's right, I was there, too, for six months. Took Dylan with me. At first, I ain't gonna lie, it was good." The similarities between this woman and Susan Lawson were uncanny. "I stopped using, and Dylan, who was on the wrong track, straightened up. But then that girl came along, and they said that Dylan touched her. It was a lie. Dylan told me so. He said they don't like him because he was caught using a phone and wanted him out."

"Did they kick him out?" Chase asked, recalling how Elijah told him that everyone was free to go as they pleased.

"*Ha*," the woman laughed bitterly. "You know, they say that they're all about this perfect society or whatever? But their idea of perfect don't include people like me and Dylan. They saw we don't got no money to give *'em*, so they gave us the worst job: cleaning the shitter. But we did it, you know? I ain't too proud to clean a shitter. Made Dylan do the same thing. Other people got promoted, got to work outside in the fields, but not us. And then that girl came along. She snuck the cell phone in, and Dylan used it. She knew she was gonna get in trouble, so she made up that sick story about Dylan touching her. After that, ain't nobody would talk to us. It got so bad that at one point we were working twenty-hour days wiping up people's shit and piss. Couldn't hack it anymore, so we left. The moment we got home? That asshole cop came by and grabbed Dylan."

"What asshole cop?" Chase asked, an idea forming in her brain.

"Trent something. I don't fucking know. Anyway, I tried to tell him that Dylan didn't do nothing, but he didn't believe me. Got two years in juvie for something he didn't do. When he got out, he was different. Quiet, you know? I asked him what happened, but he didn't say. But I saw the marks. He had cigarette burns on his arms and chest." The woman shuddered at this, and then readjusted her grip on the door.

"How did he die?" Chase asked.

"They killed him." An uncomfortable apathy had crept into the woman's tone.

"Who did?" Chase asked, bluntly.

The woman looked at Chase as if she had some sort of syndrome, which was a difficult expression to convey given the fact that she was high.

"Those assholes at the Path to Eden."

To this point, the story had been fairly predictable. Dylan molests the girl and he's shunned. Eventually, they have no choice but to leave the Path, and the minute they do, he gets thrown in jail. Other inmates hear about what he did and decide to enact their own brand of punishment. But this? The Path *killing* Dylan once he got out? That wasn't part of the script.

"I found Dylan with a needle in his arm. But the thing is, he didn't use. *Never*. I called that cop, the one that was here the day we left the cult? You wanna know how long it took for him to come pick up Dylan's body?"

Chase shook her head.

"Four days. *Four days* I was here with my dead son in the apartment before anybody showed up. I told the cop that Dylan didn't take drugs, that someone had done this to him, but they didn't even look for fingerprints."

"It was the same cop? Trent Bain?"

The woman squinted.

"Yeah, that's him."

"How do you know that the Path was behind your son's death?" Tate asked.

"You deaf? I said my son never used drugs. He had problems, sure, but drugs ain't one of them."

"I understand," Chase said, "but how do you know the Path to Eden was behind it? Based on what you said, it doesn't seem like he made many friends behind bars."

"Dylan told me that these bastards wearing bags were following him around. And the day he died? He called me at work, left a message on my cell phone. Said that they were harassing them, that they wouldn't leave them alone. He tried to tell him that he didn't do nothing, that was all a mistake, that it was all because of that stupid *fucking* cell phone. They did it. I know they did."

Chase internalized this information.

"I'm sorry for your loss," Tate said.

"So am I."

The woman slammed the door in their faces. Within seconds, Chase heard the sound of a lighter flicking inside the apartment.

Chapter 24

"LOOKS LIKE THE PATH TO Eden wasn't keen on Dylan spoiling their view of utopia. I guess turning the other cheek isn't big in the LDS community," Tate said once they were back in their rental. "You think that Dylan actually did something to that girl?"

"How should I know?" Chase said rather harshly.

Take shrugged.

"I dunno, I thought you might have some insight."

"The more important question is do you think that the Path was behind Dylan's death? Because if that's the case, I see a trend here."

"How should I know?" Tate shot back.

Chase ignored her partner's tone.

"Well, to be fair, it does kinda fit with this whole MO, the idea of cleansing the world of evil."

"That's not exactly what Elijah Kane said."

"Yeah, but it was what he implied, right?"

"I see what you're doing, Chase."

"Which is?"

"Trying to fit this whole measles thing into a narrative that I don't believe we understand the half of yet."

Chase had a scathing retort ready but was interrupted by her phone.

It was Linus.

"What do you have for us, Linus?"

"You were right, Elijah Kane has an account at a Rite Aid in Harlowton, Montana. I couldn't figure out for what, but it appears to be a recurring one."

Chase snapped her fingers.

"Bingo—take us there, Tate." And then to Linus, she said, "We just met with Dylan Cott's mother. Apparently, he's dead—thanks for the heads up, by the way. Cause of death likely listed as a drug overdose, but she suspects foul play. I need to know what's on that police report and who filed it. Is it possible to find the name of the girl he was convicted of molesting?"

"The first I can do, but find a name? Not going to be easy. You remember a couple years back when that MMA fighter was charged with murdering his uncle?"

"No."

"Well, anyways, the guy's uncle was arrested for abuse of a minor. Nobody knew who the minor was, but apparently, the MMA guy paid off some person in court records. Turns out, it was his uncle. Someone mysteriously posted bail for the scumbag, and he ended up dead hours later. It's no secret who killed him."

Tate stated the obvious.

"The MMA fighter."

"Yep. Anyways, after that case, they keep the names of minors who were abused under lock and key. I'll do my best, but I don't know if I'll be able to find it."

"Just do what you can, Linus."

"At your—"

Chase hung up.

Tate punched the address of the Rite Aid into the GPS.

"What do you expect to find there?" he asked as he started to drive.

"Not what, but *who*."

***

"You think that Elijah will be more willing to talk to us outside the compound?" Tate asked, clearly not sure what they were doing parked across the street from the Rite Aid.

"I don't think so," Chase admitted. "People like Elijah don't want to leave their comfortable little area where they hold all the power. At the compound, at the Path to Eden, Elijah is revered. He comes out here, even to a small town like Harlowton, and he's looked at with skepticism."

"So, you don't expect him to come get his stuff?"

"No, I don't. I think he'll get someone to do it for him. And, yes, I'm hoping that whoever it is is more receptive to our questions out here, out from under the watchful eye and protection of Elijah Kane."

As they waited, Tate received a phone call from Dr. Mason.

"Agent Abernathy, it's Dr. Mason. I have yet to identify the children in the truck—like I said before, the fingerprints aren't in any system. But I did perform DNA analysis and I discovered that three of them are related."

Chase's eyes widened.

"What do you mean *related*?" she asked.

"Three of the six were brothers."

Chase pictured the kid on the ground, his fingers digging into the dirt.

"Shit," she muttered.

"Before you go, there's one more thing," Dr. Mason followed up. "Dr. Niccolo has completed more tests. She believes that while the virus is more aggressive, it doesn't appear to be any heartier."

"Meaning?" Chase asked.

"Meaning that you need to come in close contact with someone who is infected to contract the virus. It doesn't appear as if it can survive on surfaces for very long."

Chase was so accustomed to receiving bad news following good, that she said nothing.

"... Agents?"

"Anything else?" Tate asked.

"That's it."

"Thanks, Dr. Mason."

Tate had only just hung up the phone before he suddenly reached over and pointed.

"Look!"

It wasn't hard to spot the woman in the crowd. She was wearing a burlap sack-type dress, and she was walking briskly across the parking lot toward the Rite Aid. Tate started to get out of the car, but Chase stopped him.

"Let me handle this," she said, looking her partner directly in the eyes.

Tate hesitated and then nodded.

"I'll be right back Keep the car running."

Chapter 25

CHASE PRETENDED TO INSPECT A bottle of contact lens solution while she kept her ears open, and her focus directed at the prescription counter.

She was unsurprised to see that the woman who had come into the Right Aid was the same woman Chase had seen in the garden at the Path to Eden with the dark hair and thick eyebrows.

"Pick up for Mr. Kane," she said softly.

The man behind the counter nodded.

"Just a moment."

He retreated into the back, and Chase watched as the woman waited impatiently, shifting her weight from one foot to another. She looked nervous, concerned.

When the prescription finally arrived, the woman paid with cash, which Chase found curious because Elijah had mentioned that they only dealt in trade. Besides, wasn't money part of the industrial machine? Isn't money something they should abhor like cell phones and social media?

It is, after all, the root of all evil.

Chase waited for the woman to exit and was about to approach when she realized that she wasn't walking back the way she'd come. Instead, after glancing around surreptitiously, she disappeared down the side of the building.

Chase, moving more cautiously now, followed.

The woman went directly to a payphone, and after her eyes darted in every direction a second time, she slid several coins into the slot.

Brow lowering in confusion, Chase leaned against the wall and listened.

"Beth, have you seen the boys?"

Chase could only hear one side of the conversation, but the tremor in the woman's voice was telling enough.

"They didn't show up yet? I'm worried. They should be there by now." The woman waited, nodded, and then said, "I know, I know. It's just that... there were these cops who came—no, not cops, but FBI agents? And they were asking about kids. I just have a bad feeling about this." There was a prolonged pause, during which the woman twirled her finger around the metal cable connecting the receiver to the payphone. "Okay. Okay, yes. Yes of course. Thank you, Beth."

The woman hung up and when she turned around, Chase made sure that she was standing directly in front of her.

The woman cried out and dropped the white prescription bag.

"I'm sorry," she said. And then her eyes met Chase's and recognition swept over her features.

"I—I can't talk to you."

Chase deliberately looked at the payphone.

"Why not? Did Elijah tell you not to speak to us?" *Us* now because Tate had joined her.

I thought I told you to wait in the car?

"I—"

"I thought you weren't supposed to use phones?" The woman's eyes dropped, and Chase saw tears silently fall down her cheeks.

"Please," the woman whimpered, bending down to pick up the bag. "Elijah needs his insulin and I have to get back. He can't know about this. He gets... he gets angry."

"We're not going to stop you," Chase said. She and Tate parted, and the woman quickly started to scamper away.

Chase waited for her to take several steps, before adding, "But I couldn't help but overhear your conversation on the phone. Ms....?"

The woman stopped and looked back at them. Her tears flowed freely now.

Chase got a sinking feeling in her gut.

"My name is Natasha. Do you know something? Do you know something about my boys?"

That feeling in Chase's stomach, which began as a knot, was now a fist twisting her intestines, kneading them, palpating them painfully.

Under other circumstances, Chase would have spoken more softly and with compassion. But sometimes ripping the band-aid off was the only way to proceed.

"I'm not sure," she answered honestly. "Unless of course, you have three sons?"

Natasha didn't say anything, she just dropped to her knees.

And then the woman started to wail.

Chapter 26

CHASE DIDN'T FEEL COMFORTABLE TAKING Natasha to the MBI command center that agent Trent Bain had set up. She was still wary of his involvement in this case, especially considering what Dylan Lynn Cotts' mother had told them. Chase also didn't like the idea of other members of the Path to Eden knowing that the woman had spoken to the FBI.

And because of Natasha's distinctive look, this ruled out the idea of going to a coffee shop or café, no matter how private. That left only their hotel room. They sequestered the woman inside, who had since stopped crying and had gone silent.

They sat her down on a chair, and Tate offered a glass of water which she readily accepted.

"What happened to my boys?" Natasha whimpered.

Telling a wife that her husband was dead, a husband who was probably responsible for the deaths of six kids, was one thing. Telling a mother that her three boys had died from a horrible disease was completely different.

"How old were your boys?" Chase asked. She winced at her use of the past tense.

"Fourteen, eleven, and nine. Please, if you know something, you have to tell me. You *have* to," the woman begged.

"When's the last time you saw them?"

Chase's own throat was parched, and she wished that Tate had given her water, as well.

"Two days ago. They are being shipped to a sister institution in Wyoming, the Garden of Light. They were gonna learn some new farming techniques because our food stores are getting low and winter will be here before..." Natasha broke down and started to sob into her hands, and Chase felt woman's pain. When Dean Jardine had taken Felix, she feared the worst. She feared that he'd been brutally murdered after being raped by the man and filmed to be sold as part of his snuff film collection.

Even so, Chase had held out hope that he was still alive. And this turned out to be true.

The possibility that the three boys, the ones that Dr. Mason had indicated were brothers, were *not* Natasha's children was low.

And with each additional question, this likelihood approached absolute zero.

"Did they leave alone?"

"I don't—I don't think so. There were some other kids that went with them. Lex and Rayne. Maybe even Donnie. Please, tell me there okay."

Chase took a deep breath and peeked at her partner.

Tate understood what she wanted and took out his phone.

"I'm gonna show you some pictures, Natasha," he said in the most somber voice she'd ever heard him use. "I'm going to warn you, though, they are graphic."

The woman let out a chocking sound but nodded.

Tate flashed his phone in front of her face. Natasha looked closely and then shook her head. Tate flicked to the next photo.

"Natasha, is this your son?"

Chase couldn't see the picture, but she didn't have to to know the answer. Natasha's face seemed to implode, all the bones disintegrating into a fine powder.

The abject pain was so great that Chase felt an urge to hold the woman. Call it maternal instinct, call it whatever you want, but when someone was in this much agony, it did something to you, to your soul.

But when she went to stand, Tate firmly indicated to remain put.

Natasha's anguish continued for a full minute before she ran out of breath and was forced to stop crying.

"Matthew," Natasha managed between sobs. "My poor Matthew."

Tate put a comforting arm on the woman's back.

"What happened?" Natasha asked when she regained enough composure to say more than just a few words. "What's wrong with his face?"

This comment was telling. It indicated that two days prior to being discovered in the back of the truck, Matthew had shown no signs of infection.

Just like Michael Lawson.

"Natasha, were your sons immunized?" Rheumy eyes shot at Tate. It was clear that she didn't understand the question, so Chase clarified.

"Did your sons have any vaccines after they were born? Measles, mumps, rubella? MMR?"

Chase remembered taking Felix for his shots and doing the same for Georgina after she'd gained custody of the girl.

"No. No, Elijah said that they didn't need any vaccinations. He said that God will look out for them, that if we just followed the Path, they wouldn't get sick. Oh, God… oh, God…"

Chase clenched her fists tightly.

Elijah Kane is responsible for these kids' deaths. Whether or not he infected them with the virus was irrelevant.

This whole Path to Eden bullshit had cost at least seven people their lives. Chase vowed to make Elijah pay for what he'd done.

"They… my boys were sick?"

Chase chose her words carefully, not sure how much she wanted to reveal to Natasha.

"Yes," she said at last. "We believe that your sons died from a measles infection."

Natasha gasped and covered her mouth. Her face was a mess now, all of that virgin allure that she'd had, the color in her cheeks from working outside, was gone.

"I'm sorry," Tate said, still rubbing Natasha's back gently. "I'm really sorry."

"How did this happen?"

"We don't know," Tate stated. "Like I said, they died from a measles infection. You mentioned that they were off to another institution?"

He was trying to keep the conversation moving, allowing less time for his words to sink in.

Natasha nodded.

"Who sent them?"

"Elijah."

Chase ground her teeth.

"I can't—I can't believe this. Can I see them? Can I see my boys?"

"Not right now," Tate said. "We don't want you to get sick, too."

"I've been vaccinated," Natasha said with a hearty nod. "I was vaccinated before I joined the Path. That means I'm safe, right? *Right?*"

"We're just being careful," Chase said. "You'll get to see them. But not right now."

Natasha suddenly rocketed to her feet and grabbed the prescription bag off the table.

"I have to go," she stated. "I have to bring Elijah his insulin."

A moment ago, the woman's face had been a mask of grief and despair. Now it had hardened into something almost unrecognizable. Chase was familiar with this response and had experienced it herself on several occasions. Sometimes, when a tragedy is so powerful, your mind simply fails to wrap itself around the truth. For a while, you existed in a sort of purgatory, believing that the horrible news you'd just heard was a dream. But as time passed, and your kids never reappeared, maybe this happened after the funeral, maybe even longer, a month, maybe two later, reality came crashing back down.

Natasha went to the door and Tate attempted to stop her.

"Out of my way. I have to go," she said angrily. "He needs his medication."

"Natasha, your sons are dead."

"You *lie*. Elijah told me you'd lie. He said that you guys would do everything in your power to stop us because you're jealous."

Chase was surprised by the venom in the woman's voice.

"We're telling you the truth," Chase said forcefully. "Your sons died yesterday morning from a measles infection. I'm very sorry for what you must be going through, but we're not lying."

For a second, it appeared as if Natasha was on the verge of accepting this. Then she shook her head and grabbed the doorknob.

"Liars," she hissed. This time, Tate let her go.

They watched her walk across the parking lot, her head held high.

"Should we stop her?" Tate asked as they both stared through the open motel room door.

Chase considered their options.

This had gone far worse than she'd hoped. Best case scenario had been that in revealing the tragedy that had befallen her children, Natasha would tell them about Elijah, about the virus, about his master plan to cleanse the world.

She'd done none of this.

Now, they were at great risk of Natasha going back and letting Elijah what she'd found out. Not only did this have disastrous consequences for Natasha herself, but it put all other kids living in the compound in jeopardy.

They could stop her, but then what? If they kept Natasha sequestered, then Elijah wouldn't get his medicine and figure out that something was up.

Then what would he do?

Would he infect more children, and send them out to the world to spread the disease?

Chase made a snap decision.

"Let her go."

Tate looked at her.

"You sure?"

"No," Chase answered honestly. "But unless you have a—" her phone rang. "Linus? We have more information for that warrant. We—"

"Chase, we got him," Linus said excitedly.

"Got who?" she asked.

"Michael Lawson. He just called his wife from a phone outside of Billings, Montana. He said he was making a run for the border. You need to get there *quick.*"

Chase and Tate didn't need to be told twice; they were already on their way to the car, thoughts of Natasha and her three dead boys momentarily forgotten.

Chapter 27

Even though Chase was remiss to do so, they had no choice but to reach out to Trent Bain to ask him to help intercept Michael Lawson.

The man sounded smug on the phone, but agreed, probably relieved that he finally had something substantial to do.

And Trent had come through. A Montana Highway Patrol officer had pulled Michael Lawson over just sixty miles from the Canadian border.

According to the cop, Michael had tried to run, but he didn't get far. The man was fat, and he'd tripped and fallen. He was now safely and securely handcuffed and, on his way, back to the MBI in the back of a police car.

Chase had given Trent Bain explicit instructions to wait until they arrived before speaking to Mr. Lawson, but unfortunately, by the time they entered the interview room, Trent was already interrogating him.

"Just tell us you got the kids, Michael. You do that, and I'll make sure you are safe in solitary. If others find out—"

Chase opened the door, her face red with fury.

"Trent, can I talk to you outside?"

Trent looked at her, as did Michael. The latter was overweight by a good twenty to thirty pounds but held most of this excess fat in his abdomen. He had a surprisingly lean face and a full head of greasy brown hair.

"I'm in the middle of an interview here," Trent said. He placed both hands on the table as if to physically root himself to the room.

"Now," Tate reinforced.

Scowling, Trent brushed past Chase and left the room with Tate.

She stayed behind.

Instead of speaking to the suspect, she pulled out her phone and scrolled without purpose. Eventually, Michael Lawson couldn't handle the suspense.

"Who are you?" he asked.

Chase didn't answer.

"Whoever you are, I'm going to tell you the same thing I just told him. I had no idea what was in the truck. I never saw, never even drove it. Someone must have stolen it."

Chase let the man ramble.

"I swear, I had no clue. There were dead kids in there? What the fuck? And someone told my wife I was dead? Hello? *Hello*? Can you say something?"

A response came to this last query, but it wasn't from Chase; there was an angry shout from the hallway. When Michael's ears perked, she finally decided that now was the time to speak.

"Michael Lawson, my name is Agent Adams with the FBI."

The man's eyelids retracted.

"FBI? What the hell! I didn't do nothin'."

"If I had a dollar every time some asshole said that to me, I'd have retired years ago."

"It's true," Michael pleaded.

"I'm sure it is. But let's start this again, shall we? This time I strongly suggest you refrain from lying."

"I'm not lying!" He was bordering on yelling now. "*I'm not!*"

"You are," Chase said. She was deliberately matching the man's intensity with calmness. If he shouted, she was going to whisper. "Your truck wasn't stolen. Now, to be honest with you, I don't know if you knew what was inside that truck, and I hope to hell you didn't, but that doesn't change the fact that you did drive to the Path to Eden to pick up the deadly cargo.

And then you drove to meet up with your ex-celly Bob Santelli. There you swapped the cars and passed the job on to him."

"I—"

"That is what I know," she said in a tiny voice. "Those are facts. Now, be very careful about what you say next. If you lie to me just once, I will pass you over to Trent Bain. And I'm pretty sure that you know what kind of reputation the man has. Especially for people who harm children."

Chase was overreaching here, using information she'd gleaned from Dylan Lynn Cott's mother, but it seemed to do the trick.

Michael crossed his arms, and she could almost see the gears behind his eyes working, trying to find a way out of this.

Sorry, bud, there isn't one.

Chase pushed a little harder.

"How many times have you been in prison, Michael?"

"Four."

"Four times. And how did you enjoy your time behind bars?"

The man made a face and shrugged.

"Let me ask you something, if you go to prison for murdering six young boys, how do you think your time behind bars will go? Not only are you a repeat offender, but I'll make sure that every single person in the prison knows exactly the reason why you're being locked up. I'll also have my friend Trent Bain talk to the guards and make sure they know that you deserve to be in gen pop and not isolated. You're a social person, Michael, I could tell the moment I stepped in here. And you deserve to be around others. Others like *you*."

She saw fear flash in the man's eyes.

"Okay, now that you understand the gravity of your current situation." There was another shout from outside, but Chase kept on rolling as if it never happened. "Let's start from the beginning. I'll tell you what I know, and then you tell me what I want to know. Got it?" The man pursed his lips. "Good. I know that you went to the Path to Eden to pick up the cargo. As I said earlier, I'll assume, at least for now, that you didn't know exactly what the cargo was, but you must've known something was up. I mean, why else would you get your delinquent buddy Bob Santilli to take over the delivery?"

"I didn't know." Michael had calmed down somewhat, and Chase adjusted her tone accordingly.

"Right. So why did you give the job to Bob? Is it because you're lazy? Or maybe you just felt bad for your buddy who was in desperate need of cash?"

The man started to nod, but Chase didn't let him.

"Don't lie—don't lie to me, Michael. I spoke to your wife—she said she expected you to be gone a few days." Chase pictured the woman smoking her cigarettes and flipping her the bird. "You want to know how she reacted when we told her you were dead? She shrugged, basically said that it was easier to cook for just one, anyway."

Michael Lawson's lips curled into a frown.

"But that's a chat for a different day. What I want you to do, right now, is tell me one thing. If you tell me who at the Path to Eden paid you to pick up the package, I'll make sure that Trent follows through on his promise to keep you segregated from the other prisoners."

"I don't know," Michael Lawson said.

Chase turned toward the door.

"I'm serious, I don't know. They called me on this shitty phone and their voice was all messed up. They said they'd give me 10k to make stops across the country. Deliver six packages. I didn't what the packages were."

This didn't make sense, and they both knew it.

What was he supposed to do when he got to these locations? Just open the back and close his eyes as one of the infected kids crawled out?

No, they told him what the package was, alright.

The other lie was that they only paid him $10,000. Michael Lawson lived in a shit hole, but $10,000 wasn't enough money even for someone like him to get involved in something *this* fucked up.

"I'm thinking more like, they gave you $10,000 for each kid you dropped off."

Michael held fast.

"I didn't know it was kids."

"Sure. Just like you don't know who asked you to deliver them, right?"

Now the man got mad and slammed his palms on the table. The second he did that the arguing in the hallway came to an abrupt stop. Then the door about and Tate stormed in.

"I swear to you, they used this fucking Deep Throat thing on the phone. Never said their name."

"But it was the Path to Eden, right?"

"What the fuck is the Path to Eden?"

He was angry now, so Chase lowered her voice.

"A cult with a huge church and several acres of gardens."

Michael finally relented.

"It was close to there, yeah. The pick-up location. But, I'm telling you, I didn't know it was kids."

This was all they were going to get out of the man.

Chase grabbed Tate's arm and spoke just loud enough for Michael to hear.

"Tell Trent to book him. Tell him to let every single person behind bars know what Michael did."

"Hey!" Michael yelled as Trent, who had also overheard, entered the interview room. "Hey, you said you would—"

"I lied," Chase exited the room, followed closely by Tate.

"He give you anything of value?" her partner asked.

"He did. He gave me enough to secure that warrant to search the Path to Eden. And if it's not enough, well, fuck it, I'm going in anyways, I don't care what you or Trent Bain have to say about it."

Chapter 28

DEREK APPEARED SUDDENLY, RED-FACED, AND out of breath.

"What's wrong?" Elijah asked. He shooed the woman whose ear he'd been whispering in, a tall, skinny blond in charge of making bread.

"Can I speak with you?"

Elijah encouraged the woman who was still lingering to get a move on.

She hurried away.

"What's up, Derek?"

Derek swept his hair behind his ears.

"You remember how you mentioned that you had something special planned for an upcoming service? Something that you wanted to tell all the parishioners?"

Elijah's eyes narrowed and he thought back to his conversation on the cell phone earlier in the day.

Derek couldn't have possibly overheard, could he?

"What about it?" Elijah said sharply.

"Well, I was in storage, doing an inventory of our food stocks and one of the kids came in. Saw how little we had and ran off before I could get to him."

Derek had a strange expression on his face as he spoke, one that Elijah had difficulty interpreting.

"And?" He was annoyed at how banal and protracted this story was becoming.

This is why you pulled me away from the blond? Fuck *the food stocks.*

"The boy told his mom and there are murmurs about how we don't have enough to get through the winter."

"The *winter*?" Elijah looked skyward as he said this. It was getting dark and without the sun beating down on them, the air was chilly. But during the day, it was still intensely hot out. "The winter is months off. Maybe if the kids didn't spend their time wandering in places they shouldn't be and instead focus on their jobs we wouldn't have a shortage problem."

Derek swallowed hard and nodded.

"I know, I know. But the rumors—"

"Tonight." Elijah straightened as he made up his mind. Derek waited for him to continue, and Elijah took his time. "I want you to gather everyone in the church tonight. We're going to have a special mass."

"I think… I think that's a good idea."

Oh, you don't know the half of it.

"Mandatory attendance. I want everyone inside. Every last person. Do you understand?"

Derek nodded.

Tonight was sooner than Elijah wanted, but he still had a few hours.

That was more than enough to prepare for his escape.

He'd grown tired of this. All the responsibility… it wasn't what he'd signed up for.

But that was okay because it was all about to change.

Elijah's mind turned inward, returning to his time at the LDS.

There, he'd just been a nobody. Here, he was a God.

And Gods had to act in a Godly manner. They were forced to make tough decisions, to make sacrifices.

Elijah started to grin.

The devil finds work for idle hands.

Yeah, that was the saying he was thinking of. Did it even fit?

Maybe. Who cares.

Elijah had more important things to worry about now.

"Yeah," he said. "Gather everyone in the church *tonight*."

Chapter 29

THE WARRANT WAS ISSUED IN under an hour. One hour after that, the entire sting operation was set up and ready to go. They purposely employed the local police department, and Billings' SWAT offered to help out. They used the photos from Chase's drone flight to plan their attack.

Tate was leading the charge. Dr. Niccolo was there as well, providing insight and medical knowledge prior to infiltrating the compound. The only person who was missing was Trent Bain, who they'd left behind to take care of Michael Lawson.

"There are at least four entrances and exits to the main church, where we believe that Elijah Kane is most likely to be holed up in," Tate said, giving her an appreciative nod. Chase was the one who had suggested that Kane would have his own, separate sleeping quarters. She knew people like him, knew what he wanted, what got men like him off.

Power.

"The team will split up into four groups, with the main firepower focused on the front and rear exits." Tate pointed at these areas in the image and then indicated the exits near the ends of the two wings, the Western and Eastern sides that made up the main compound's U-shaped structure.

"This is the man were looking for," Tate said, pulling out another image and laying it on the table. Unlike the pictures taken by the drone, this was not a photograph. They had Linus scour the Internet for photos of Elijah Kane, even back in his LDS days, but they'd come up empty. The best they could do was commission an artist's rendition, a police artist's sketch based on both Tate and Chase's memory of meeting the man. Admittedly, it wasn't great, but Chase didn't think that they would have a problem identifying Elijah. He would be the one that the others would try to protect.

That and his robe made him easily distinguishable from the rest.

"Got it?" This was met with nods and murmurs of agreement.

One SWAT team member, a burly man with a handlebar mustache, spoke up.

"What's with the masks?" he asked, indicating the gas masks that had been laid out on an adjacent table.

Tate addressed Helen Niccolo.

"Dr. Niccolo?"

The woman stepped forward.

"We believe that there might be a biological weapon hidden somewhere in the compound."

These were tough men, tough men who had seen a lot, tough men who lived for moments like this.

Still, there was a collective intake of breath. Just the word biological weapon brought up memories of the wars in Iraq and Afghanistan. Such weapons might never have been discovered, but the threat of them was real enough.

"The biological weapon in question is a weaponized measles virus," Dr. Niccolo continued.

This was unexpected and Chase saw several confused looks.

"That's the reason why we needed you to provide your vaccination records," Tate said.

"Measles?" The man with the handlebar mustache asked, incredulous.

Tate nodded.

"Measles. But a very aggressive form. I won't go into details, and I won't guarantee you that the vaccination you received will prevent you from becoming infected. The masks, if worn properly, should do the job, however."

Once more, Tate indicated Dr. Niccolo.

"That's right, your masks are more than capable of keeping the virus out."

Chase listened with half an ear as she took a step back from the group. From where they were situated, they couldn't quite see the compound through the trees, but they should have been able to hear it.

Except it was deathly quiet.

The only noises piercing the night air originated from wildlife.

Chase didn't like it. The silence didn't sit right with her.

As they continued to discuss their plan, Chase got her drone out again. Nobody noticed her slipping the goggles over her head. As the drone took off, she heard Tate say, "The element of surprise should be in our hands, and we need to keep it that way. No one wants a shoot out here. Elijah Kane is like the head of a snake. Remove him from the situation, and there shouldn't be any resistance. In and out, no bloodshed—that's our goal."

Chase flew the drone a little lower than earlier in the day. Being nighttime, it would barely be visible. Just in case, she had used electrical tape to cover the blinking landing lights.

She expected to see several people out and about, tending to the plants, the animals, even walking around. Maybe sitting around a campfire singing Kumbaya or some other such bullshit.

But she saw nobody.

Tate fielded a few more questions and then instructed the men to get ready. Masks were snapped on, guns were checked, and then heavy boots started toward the compound.

Something's not right here.

The men appeared in her goggles, moving at alarming speed as they spread out.

Chase, feeling dread beginning to sink in, flew the drone toward the church.

Somewhere far away, back near her body, she heard a car pull up.

Tate cursed under his breath.

"What you doing here?" her partner said as she lowered the drone further and then zoomed in on the window of the church.

"You think that you're going to go in there and grab my half-brother and I'm not gonna be a part of it?"

It was Trent Bain.

"You promised you would recuse yourself, Trent," Tate said. "We have concrete evidence the kids are from the Path to Eden."

"Well, fuck that. You promised to keep me apprised of what was going on, and no one even thought to give me a call? Tell me that you're about to storm the compound? How did you get a warrant anyway?"

"You need to leave. You need to leave *now.*"

"I'm not going anywhere. Give me one of those masks." There was a tussle and Chase was about to remove the goggles when she spotted something strange. The interior of the church was pitch black. And then she saw the faintest flicker of a flame.

The church wasn't dark, it was *full*.

Everyone was in the church. Hundreds of them, squashed together so tightly that they were blocking out the light.

Something that Tate had just said echoed in her brain.

The element of surprise.

"Guys," she said huskily.

"You're not going anywhere, Trent. Back the fuck down."

"Or what? You gonna make me?"

"Guys, we gotta pull them back."

***

"Make space, make space," Elijah instructed. Despite how tight everyone was inside the church, no one dared step up onto the stage which, aside from him, was completely empty.

Derek was supposed to be by his side, but after corralling the gardeners, he'd disappeared.

Fuck him, Elijah thought. *He doesn't matter. None of them do.*

"I'm guessing you all are wondering why I've gathered you hear tonight."

A series of murmurs filled the church.

"I know this is a bit odd, that it's not typical. But that's the thing, *gardeners*, times are changing. Even for us, for the Path, which has stayed true for so long, there comes a time when we need to adapt."

Out of the corner of his eye, he saw someone step onto the stage to his far right.

Elijah tried to motion her away as he continued speaking.

"And many of you aren't going to understand the reasons why I have made certain decisions on your behalf."

The person who was moving across the stage toward him now was a woman, he saw.

"Go back down there," he hissed at her. She didn't listen. "Go on, *shoo*."

It was Natasha, a woman that he'd slept with a few months back.

She'd been a terrible lay, pure starfish and not much else.

What the hell does she want?

Others had noticed the commotion and began talking among themselves.

Elijah cleared his throat.

"But I assure you, while this decision did not come lightly, it is critical to the Path's future success."

Natasha continued toward him.

She had a knowing look in her eyes. But how was that possible? Natasha was just a lowly gardener.

A nobody.

She couldn't know what he'd done.

"Quiet, please. What I have to say is incredibly important." Elijah raised his voice, trying to regain control of the crowd. "And I need you all to—"

He stopped speaking when Natasha sprinted toward him.

***

"I will have you arrested for obstruction. I don't care if you're—"

Chase tore the goggles off her face and pressed the recall button on the controller.

"Guys, we need to get them back *right now*," she said with such authority that both Trent and Tate, who looked close to coming to blows, glanced over at her.

"What's going on?" Tate asked, his eyes dropping to the drone goggles she held in one hand.

"They know," Chase said. "They *know*. Someone told him that were coming. Remember what Elijah said? They only do services three times a day, morning, noon, and night. There's no midnight mass. We need to get everyone out of there, now." None of the men moved, and Chase glared at her partner. "You want another Waco on our hands? You want everyone in that fucking church to become infected with the measles virus? *No?* Then call them back!"

Tate raced to a table and grabbed a radio. And then he started barking orders.

There was some dissension, but eventually, all four squad leaders confirmed that they would return without interacting with anyone from the Path to Eden.

Tate glared at Trent.

"You told them. You told your half-brother," he accused. "You warned them that we were coming."

"Fuck you," Trent spat.

"No, fuck you," Tate said, and then he shoved Trent. Trent was solidly built, but he didn't expect this and stumbled. Chase tried to get in between them and stop the fight that she knew was about to break out.

But she was bumped by Trent as he lunged at Tate and was knocked to the ground. What happened next was more of a wrestling match than a fist fight.

"Stop it!" Chase screamed.

This was a mistake. As soon as Tate saw that she'd been toppled, he redoubled his efforts, flipping Trent over, and postured up.

The SWAT team arrived, and Chase turned her attention to the man with the handlebar mustache.

"Stop them!" she yelled. "Stop them!"

The man didn't hesitate, he was amped up and ready for battle and ran toward the combatants. He managed to grab Tate's arm before the first blow landed, deflected it off to one side, and then physically hauled her partner backward. Both men fell and she heard the wind being knocked out of Tate.

More men arrived on the scene. Two of them restrained Trent while it took four to hold Tate down.

"You fucking told them!" Tate hollered.

"I didn't tell anybody!" Trent yelled back. "I didn't say shit!"

A third voice joined the fray, this one belonging to Dr. Niccolo, who had managed to slink away during the fight.

"Oh my God," the woman gasped.

"What?" Chase demanded.

Dr. Niccolo didn't say anything, she just pointed. Coming down the road, was none other than Natasha, the woman whose three sons had been killed. She was wearing the same outfit she'd been sporting earlier in the day, that strange almost Mennonite-looking dress. Only there was something different about it.

It was covered in blood.

"He killed my babies," Natasha whispered. "Elijah killed my babies, so I killed him."

Part III – The Path to Eden

Chapter 30

WHILE NATASHA'S BLOODY PRESENCE SOBERED Tate, it enraged Trent.

The four men who were holding Tate now wrestled with Trent, who was shouting something incomprehensible.

Chase blocked this out and ran to Natasha. She helped the woman to her feet, inspected her quickly for wounds, and after determining that the blood wasn't hers, said, "What happened?"

Natasha looked at her with vacant eyes.

"What happened?" Chase repeated, shaking Natasha with each word.

Still nothing.

"Shit." Chase let the woman go and looked at Tate. "Call the EMT. We need to get in there, now."

The plan had been to grab Elijah and get out without a single drop of bloodshed. But plans had a tendency to go sideways, and they always had EMTs on standby.

And gone sideways it had.

Tate got on the radio and called the EMT. Within moments, two ambulances pulled up. Chase instructed the first to deal with Natasha, while she and Tate hopped in the second. Despite the now half dozen people restraining Trent, he nearly broke free and got to them.

"I need to see my brother!"

"Keep him back," Tate shouted as Chase slammed the rear doors of the EMT closed.

Chase climbed over the partition into the front seat next to the driver.

"Drive, we gotta get into the compound. *Now.*"

The EMT, who was in his early twenties, hit the gas. They narrowly avoided running over Trent who was still struggling with multiple SWAT members, and then hightailed it towards the arched entrance.

"Should I—"

"Blow through it," Chase instructed, pointing at the thin wooden barrier.

The ambulance smashed the barricade without slowing.

Chase craned her neck forward, peering into the darkness as they sped down the dirt road toward the church.

She expected the congregation to be outside, wandering around aimlessly now that their fearless leader had been killed, but she didn't see anybody.

The ambulance wasn't even fully stopped before Chase jumped out. Tate followed suit and they both rushed toward the front doors.

And then came a throng of people. They all had blank faces and were doing nothing but getting in the way.

"Move!" Chase yelled. "Move!"

Some of them obeyed and those that didn't were knocked to the ground. Their progress was stalled inside the church. They needed to get to the stage but there were just too many people blocking their path.

This left Chase with only one recourse. She pulled her gun and aimed it skyward. And then she pulled the trigger three times.

The sound of the gun going off inside the church was deafening and several people shrieked.

The flow of parishioners desperate to get out was like a tsunami, shoving Chase in the opposite direction that she wanted to go.

"Damn it," she cursed.

Tate was at her back now, pushing her forward and at last they made progress. Chase had no idea where the EMT was, but she hoped that he was making his way inside, as well.

With the crowd thinning now, they finally made it to the stage.

And then she saw him.

Elijah Kane was exactly where she thought he would be: lying on the stage next to the pulpit. Two women, young, both blond, sporting similar outfits to Natasha, blood and all, were cradling his body and wailing, their chins turned to the heavens.

"Out of the way," Chase said, as she leaped up the two steps and approached Elijah's corpse. One of the women took a step back, but the other did not, and Chase had to physically thrust her aside.

Elijah was on his back, one leg twisted awkwardly beneath him. His eyes were closed, and she couldn't detect any rise and fall of his chest.

The man was wearing dark robes and to find where he'd been injured, Chase was forced to pull them open.

He was naked beneath.

The blood was coming from two wounds on his right side, one just above his hip, and the other higher, about four inches below his nipple.

The flow of blood had ceased almost to the point of stopping. Chase pressed her hands against both lacerations as hard as she could.

"Tate?" she shouted.

Don't die on me, she thought. *Don't you fucking die on me.*

Her hands sticky with blood, Chase looked behind her.

Tate rushed to her side with the EMT in tow.

"I don't think he's breathing," she said.

The EMT dropped his black case and unzipped it. Then he took out two pads, removed the backing, and placed them on Elijah's chest.

"Hands off," he instructed, and Chase reluctantly held up her red palms.

"Clear," she said. There was a loud buzzing sound and Elijah Kane's body jumped as electricity coursed through him.

The EMT checked for a pulse and then shocked him again.

"Is he alive?" Chase asked desperately.

The EMT didn't answer. After a series of chest compressions, he delivered a more powerful shock, one so intense that Chase felt a burst of static electricity even though she was no longer touching Elijah's body.

"Is he alive?" Chase shouted again.

The EMT grabbed a pre-loaded syringe next and held it up to the light.

"God dammit, just tell me if he's alive," Chase demanded.

The EMT squirted clear fluid into the air.

"He's alive. Barely, but he's alive."

Chapter 31

CHASE AND TATE WERE WAITING outside the operating room when the surgeon finally appeared. The man looked exhausted, and even taking off his scrub cap to wipe sweat from his brow with the back of a hairy forearm seemed laborious.

"Did he make it?" Chase asked desperately. "Did Elijah pull through?"

The doctor eyed both her and Tate before saying, "Mr. Kane has a punctured lung and a lacerated kidney. We managed to stem the bleeding, but the main complication is severe blood loss."

"But did he make it?" Chase demanded. She felt Tate's hand brush the small of her back.

They needed him to be alive. Elijah might be responsible for the bodies in the back of the truck, and he might be an egotistical serial philanderer, among other things, but she didn't peg him as a genetic mastermind.

They needed Elijah to tell them where the Path to Eden was keeping the modified measles virus and who had engineered it.

"He's alive," the doctor informed them, his expression remaining unchanged. "But his brain was deprived of oxygen for nearly six minutes. We're keeping him in an induced coma for the foreseeable future, perfusing his body with fresh blood to see how his brain reacts. He's going for an EEG scan now to determine if he has any brain activity left."

"Fuck," Chase cursed. "*Fuck!*"

Tate remained calm.

"Thank you, doctor," he said with a nod. "We have a Billings police officer on his way. He's to accompany Elijah at all times. If the man comes to, no one outside of you and your medical staff is to speak with him. This includes family and other law enforcement agencies. If Elijah wakes up, you need to call as soon as possible."

The doctor agreed and Tate slipped him his business card. And then he left, presumably to catch up on much-needed sleep.

Chase felt like doing the same.

She reached up and massaged her forehead.

"I fucked up," she said softly. "God damn it, I fucked up."

Tate frowned.

"No, you didn't," he assured her. "You had no way of knowing that Natasha was capable of something like this."

Tate was only trying to comfort her, but it wasn't helping.

Of all the scenarios that had run through Chase's head when she'd instructed Tate to let Natasha go, the woman stabbing and attempting to kill Elijah Kane was not one of them.

But she *should* have known.

You had no way of knowing that Natasha was capable of something like this.

This was a complete and utter lie.

Chase knew exactly what lengths a mother scorned would go to to protect or avenge their child.

Tate put his arm around her shoulder and gave her a squeeze.

"SWAT should be finishing up with the search of the compound, now. We should head to the command center, see what they've found."

Chase nodded, but she didn't leave the room right away. Instead, she moved closer to the glass and pressed her hands up against it as she peered into the operating room.

Elijah Kane was hooked up to a respirator, his eyes still taped shut from the surgery. Every few seconds, the ventilator clicked, and the man's lungs expanded.

Chase felt no sympathy for him.

Elijah had deliberately infected six kids with a virus he knew would kill them and had attempted to infect hundreds, if not thousands, of others.

And why?

Because he wanted to cleanse this world of our technological sins?

Chase should have been satisfied that they'd finally caught their man, but she wasn't.

If anything, she was disappointed.

Tate gently pulled her away from the glass and guided her toward the door.

"C'mon, Chase. Let's go."

***

Dr. Niccolo and the SWAT leader with the mustache had exercised the search warrant in Chase's, Tate's, and Trent's absence. And now they were back, looking worn. Dr. Mason had joined them, as well. Trent was absent—a man who identified himself as Agent William Van Horven from the MBI informed them that there was an internal investigation into Trent's actions and that he'd been suspended while this was ongoing.

Chase scoffed at this.

If it were up to her, Trent would have been immediately relieved of duty and arrested.

"As per your request, Agent Adams," Dr. Niccolo began once they were all seated, "we have quarantined the entire compound and everyone in it. Dr. Mason's team is currently in the process of performing antigen checks on members of the Path to Eden to determine if they've been infected. So far, none of the results have come back positive. We did find a high prevalence of STIs in the community, mostly gonorrhea, but we don't believe that this is in any way related to the weaponized measles virus. Moreover, we have yet to discover vials or anything even suggestive of biological weaponry. But, as you know, the Path to Eden is a large place. It will take some time to search everywhere."

Chase frowned.

The information about the STIs didn't surprise her. She knew that people like Elijah Kane often use their position of authority to subdue and sleep with women in their congregation. It came with the territory.

"What about lab equipment?" Chase asked. Her words came out slowly—she was as exhausted as Dr. Niccolo appeared and emotionally depleted, as well.

The woman shook her head.

"We've found no evidence of lab equipment." Dr. Niccolo shuffled papers awkwardly in front of her. "Nothing that would suggest that they are capable of engineering the virus."

Chase ground her molars.

"It has to be in there somewhere. Keep looking."

"My men are going over the place," the SWAT agent said. "If anything's there, we'll find it."

"Any update on Natasha?" Chase asked.

"She's not speaking," SWAT told her. "The MBI has her in custody."

Chase was unsurprised by this, as well. When Natasha had collapsed on the ground, the woman had been reduced to a shell.

"Well, she should be heralded as a hero," Chase said absently.

William Van Horven grew visibly uncomfortable but before he could say anything, Tate spoke up.

"How are the parishioners taking the quarantine?"

With Elijah gone, Chase suspected mass confusion followed by an exodus. Once the blinders were removed from the horses, they often went wild, relishing and frolicking in their newfound freedom.

"Well," Dr. Niccolo said, "they seem to be going about business as usual. Many of them are upset about what happened to Elijah, but they maintain that they have jobs to do to keep the Path to Eden up and running. We're not telling them much, as per your recommendation, Agent Adams."

This second part came as a surprise.

Some of the gardeners fully believed in the Path's message, but most, she suspected, had been drawn into the fold by Elijah's charm. And with him gone, their desire to stay was a bit of a mystery.

Could it be that they've been indoctrinated for so long that this is the only thing they know?

Chase recalled when she'd finally found her sister and offered her her freedom.

Georgina had declined, her mind working overtime, performing mental gymnastics, and adding several layers of cognitive dissonance in order to refute the truth.

She sighed.

"What about the children?" Chase asked almost as an afterthought.

"We have identified three women who claim that their children, aged…" MBI Agent William looked down at the piece of paper in his hand, "nine, ten, and twelve, who are unaccounted for. We believe that they are most likely the parents of the three other boys who were discovered in the truck."

William's approach was business-like, matter of fact. Pretty much the exact opposite of the hothead that was Trent Bain.

"Can we confirm this? Have they been taken to identify the bodies?" Tate asked.

Dr. Mason fielded his question.

"Not as of yet. Despite Dr. Niccolo's assurances that the virus is less transmissible than we first thought, we're still exercising caution. We are prepared to wait another day or two, before bringing them to the morgue."

"The kids' names are probably Lex, Rayne, and Donnie," Chase said, recalling what Natasha had told them back in the motel room.

Uttering their names out loud brought about feelings of guilt, which was further encouraged by the modicum of relief Chase felt surge deep inside her.

Six kids had died but countless others had been saved.

Yet, as often happened with her, negative emotions swiftly drowned out any budding positive sentiments.

"What about the other kids?" she asked absently. She expected Dr. Niccolo or maybe the SWAT Agent to answer, but neither did. "The other children?" she repeated with a little more strength. "Are they safe?"

"What other children?" The man with the handlebar mustache shot back.

"The path to Eden had—what? Two-hundred fifty-plus members? Some of them had to be children. There has to be more than just the six we found in the truck."

At first, Chase was astonished that nobody had considered the safety of any additional children. But then she reminded herself that they were dealing with an ME, a scientist, and a man built to break down doors, not Poirot or Columbo.

That was hers and Tate's job: to ask questions and find answers.

To this point, Chase believed they'd done a poor job of both. And, as a result, people had died or were in a medically induced coma.

"Ah," the handlebar man said, finally catching on. "We found two kids, four and six years old."

"No evidence of infection," Dr. Mason said. "We tested them first."

He seemed proud of this.

"Just *two* other kids?" Chase asked.

Nobody seemed to share her incredulity.

"That's all we found," the handlebar man said with a shrug.

There had to be more. For a group this size, and with STIs rampant suggesting that the Path's tenets did not preclude copious amounts of sex, there had to be *many* more children.

"How long is it going to take to clear every one of infection?" Tate asked as Chase mulled these thoughts over.

"On the low side, three days. High side, a week. Maybe ten days," Dr. Mason informed them. "We're not really equipped to deal with processing this volume of samples."

Where are the other kids?

"Did you ask any of the women if they have children? Did they send them off to the sister cult for training?" she asked, remembering what Natasha had told her.

Mr. Handlebar grew uncomfortable.

"No, we just—we thought they would mention it. We can ask, though."

"Yeah, ask."

"What about media involvement?" William said.

Chase's eyes flicked to the man. Unlike Trent Bain, William's tone suggested a loathing for the industry, which she shared.

"The thing is," he continued, "some reporters are already nosing around. Somebody leaked the fact that Elijah was hospitalized and now they're asking questions."

"Let them ask. For now, I don't want anyone to speak to the media, got it?" Chase ordered. "The gag order remains in place."

William nodded and, with that, they wrapped up the formalities. With the question of missing children still lingering, Chase and Tate returned to their motel room.

They found beer in the mini-fridge and sat and drank. Chase fiddled with the tab on her can as she contemplated the day's events, wiggling it back and forth until it came free in hand.

"Something feels off about this, Tate."

Tate sipped his beer.

"I know," he agreed. "I'm just not sure if that's because we didn't find the stash of the measles virus or because of what happened to Elijah Kane."

"It's not only that," Chase said, shaking her head. "You really think that Elijah only infected six kids? If his goal was a country-wide cleanse, then he was extremely short-sighted. If I were in his shoes, I would have prepared multiple shipments, staggering them in case some trucks were discovered, and sent them in all directions. Trusting just one man, a man like Michael Lawson, seems foolish."

Take shrugged.

"Then I'm grateful that you aren't Elijah Kane."

"Tate, I'm serious."

"As am I—what do we really know about this guy, anyway? Elijah was a member of the LDS who went to university and then decided to start his own cult? Maybe the whole cleansing thing was just an accident. Maybe the kids got sick, and he wanted to ship them away, like he did with Dylan. You know how it is—a crack in utopia often leads to dystopia. These cults only work if things run perfectly. As soon as the barriers begin to break down—people start getting sick or growing hungry—they ask questions and we both know that asking questions threatens the entire fabric of their society."

A reasonable theory, one that Chase might have even gotten behind.

Except for one glaring fact.

"Who made the virus?"

Tate bit his lip and then drank from his can of beer.

"I don't know."

"I don't know, either."

Chase finished her drink and then crawled into bed.

That night, she dreamed of her sister.

Chapter 32

FOR THE FIRST TIME IN a long time, Tate was up before Chase. When she opened her eyes, she found her partner sitting in a chair and not in bed beside her.

"Couldn't sleep?"

Tate, who had been scrolling through his phone when she awoke, glanced up. His look said it all.

"Naw."

"Something still bothering you about this case, too?"

Tate nodded.

"I just filled Hampton and Stitts in on the details. They suggest wrapping things up and submitting our report. They want to see how things play out with Elijah Kane before offering recommendations to the DA."

Chase groaned and wiped sleep from her eyes.

"Yeah, I figured they would say that."

Chase rose out of bed and showered. After putting on fresh clothes, she noticed that Tate had packed up their things, including her drone.

"What do you want to do, Chase? Head back to Virginia?"

The fact that Tate asked this question was telling. If he thought things were done here, that it was all wrapped, he would already be driving them to the airport.

"I want to go back to the Path to Eden. Just one more time. Check-in, see if they've found anything else."

Tate grinned.

"I was hoping you would say that."

Chase expected the news vans that were scattered among the police cars blocking the entrance to the Path to Eden. The reporters were doing their thing, bombarding the officers with questions, but Chase was pleased that the blood-sucking leeches didn't appear to be getting the answers they so craved.

"Can you guys tell us what happened to Elijah Kane?" A woman with a ponytail that was so tight it made her eyebrows lift asked. "There are reports that he is in critical condition at Billings General."

"No comment."

"What about reports that several children have gone missing from the compound? That they're sick?"

"No comment."

Chase walked up to an officer and showed him her badge. Tate did the same.

"Excuse me? Are you with the FBI?"

Chase ignored the question as the officer led them to a table off to one side.

"Masks are required to enter the compound," he informed them.

"I know," Chase said, picking up a mask.

"Are you Chase Adams?"

Chase, shocked that someone had used her name, turned around to look at the woman who had addressed her. She was young, with short dark brown hair tucked behind ears that, like Lorraine's, were slightly too large for her head.

"What's *your* name?" Chase asked, shooting the woman's question back at her.

The reporter extended her cell phone, making sure to record everything.

"Harper Sterling, *REEL ME* news. I recognize you from photographs I've seen online. What are you doing here, Agent Adams? And what's with the masks?"

"You from New York?" Chase asked instinctively, knowing that most of the information about her life was from her time in

New York as either an NYPD officer or later as a green FBI Agent.

"LA."

"Well, you're a long way from LA, Harper. Might I suggest you go back and do a story on some social media influencer and leave the real work to us?"

Tate tugged her arm and together they walked down the dusty path to the compound. The sun was bright again today, but the mask blocked out a significant portion of its rays.

Even though the parishioners—*gardeners,* according to Lorraine—weren't permitted to leave, they weren't being prevented from doing their daily duties.

If not for the police presence and medical staff wearing masks, today would be indistinguishable from their visit yesterday.

Again, this struck Chase as odd. Cut the head off the snake and the snake was supposed to die. But this whole cult, this Path to Eden, looked more like a worm than a snake. Cut a worm in half, and both sides keep on living, oblivious to the other.

"Agent Adams." Handlebar mustache man came forward, hands on his hips.

"I'm sorry, I never got your name."

"Marshall Woods of Billings SWAT." He said proudly. "Dr. Mason is taking samples over there, while Dr. Niccolo is in the church."

"Thanks. Find anything interesting overnight?"

The man appeared disappointed.

"No, not yet." Marshall lowered his voice. "No vials or lab equipment."

Chase thanked the man again and then entered the church.

Several women were kneeling in front of pews and praying. No one had bothered cleaning up the blood on the stage, and it had coagulated into a dark brown stain. It was a surreal scene. But, to Chase, churches harbored a touch of the mystical.

Chase thought back to something Tate had said last night, about how asking questions threatens the entire fabric of their society.

She supposed this was by design.

They found Dr. Niccolo conversing with a woman off to one side and as they approached, the scientist shooed the lady away.

Both of them crossed themselves, which Chase found bizarre.

This was a woman grounded in science. How could someone dedicated to the stringent demands of scientific inquiry subscribe to beliefs that not only positioned themselves beyond scientific boundaries but also seemed to contradict them entirely?

Consider faith, for example.

The definition of the word was belief without evidence. Is that how Niccolo got her PhD or whatever other degrees she might hold? Did she ask her reviewers to disregard the shaky science and simply have faith... because she insisted?

Chase suddenly regretted listening to Trent when he'd brought the woman in.

She should have vetted Dr. Niccolo herself.

But it was too late for that now.

"Still no evidence of the virus here," Dr. Niccolo said, parroting Marshall Woods' words. Her voice was muffled behind the mask.

"So, I've heard. Let me guess, that's Elijah Kane's room up there," Chase said, pointing to the loft above the stage.

"It is. We went through all of his things, didn't come up with—"

"Thanks."

She gestured for Tate to follow her upstairs.

The door to the man's room hung ajar and Chase used the back of her sleeve to push it open all the way.

Prominently displayed in the center of the room was a large circular bed covered in plush white sheets. There was a small nightstand beside the bed, the drawers of which hung open. Clearly, SWAT or whoever else was performing the search had spent considerable time here, and with good reason. As Tate walked over to the window and pulled the drapes back, Chase proceeded to the bedside table and began rifling through its contents. She opened a notepad and saw a list of women's names—five full pages of them, maybe sixty names in total.

This explains the STIs, she thought glumly.

Disgusted, Chase tossed the book aside. The other drawers held dozens of condoms and a litany of sex toys.

What are you still doing here, gardeners? She thought with considerable disdain. *Your exalted leader was nothing more than a Class A pervert. Beat it.*

Chase was about to close the drawer when she spotted something at the bottom.

"No way," she said, picking the object up. "Tate?"

"You find something?" Tate asked, turning away from the window. When he saw what she was holding between two fingers, his chin disappeared into his neck.

"Impossible. The esteemed leader who rejects all forms of technology owns a *cell phone*?"

"Sure looks that way. Probably only uses it for porn."

Chase spotted something beneath the bed and dropped to her knees. She used the flashlight from her own phone to get a better look. The beam reflected off something metal. Thinking that it might be a gun, and wondering how the hell SWAT could have missed this or the cell phone, she reached under the bed and grabbed it.

"What the hell is that?" Tate asked.

"Don't know," she said, fiddling with the buttons of the device that looked like an old-school tape recorder.

"I don't think that's a good idea."

Chase pressed a large button on the side and said, "Why? You think there's—" She was going to say *a measles virus inside here*, but stopped suddenly.

Her voice sounded different, almost mechanical.

Chase frowned and brought the device closer to her mask.

"I wouldn't—"

"My name is Elijah Kane," she said, and both of them froze.

It was a voice changer.

"Shit, Michael Lawson said that the person on the phone sounded like a robot," Chase remarked. "I bet this is what Elijah used." She dangled the cell phone. "I bet he used *both* of these."

"Bag them," Tate said, removing two evidence bags from his pocket.

"You just walk around with those bags on you?" she asked, a hint of a smile forming on her lips. "You know what they say, *No diggity, you got bag it up*." As he spoke, Tate's eyes drifted to the nightside table and the plethora of condoms that were still visible.

"Yeah, Elijah Kane should have heeded that advice," Chase said, and her smile evaporated. She bagged the voice changer and the phone. Seconds later, her own phone started to buzz. She was startled, initially thinking that it was Elijah's device that had vibrated.

"What's up Linus?" she said. "I guess you heard the news?"

"I did, looking forward to having you guys back here soon. Just wanted to give you an update on that Dylan Lynn Cott case."

"Oh?" Chase had forgotten all about Dylan.

"Yeah, I actually found out the name of the girl he assaulted. It was a pain in the ass but by calling in some favors, I—"

Chase was in no mood for Linus' pedantic verbal meanderings.

"What's her name?"

"Ali Rennick," Linus said. "Ring a bell?"

It didn't, and Chase said as much.

"Guess it's a dead end. I'll—"

"Wait a second, Rennick?" Tate interrupted, moving closer to the phone.

"Yeah, Rennick. Two 'Ns'."

"You know it?" Chase asked.

"I think so, yeah," Tate said. "You remember when we first met Lorraine? When she brought us to the church?"

"Yes," Chase answered hesitantly. They'd only been here yesterday morning, but after everything that had happened, it felt like a decade ago.

"Remember the guy with the long gray hair who we spoke to first?"

Chase closed her eyes and pictured the man that Tate had described. She remembered that he had a surprisingly youthful face.

"Yeah, sure."

"His name was Rennick," Tate said.

Chase squinted one eye.

"You sure?"

"First name Derek?" Linus' voice came from the speaker.

"Yes, Derek? Why?" Tate asked quickly.

"Because that's the name of Ali's father on her birth certificate. Ali Rennick's father is Derek Rennick."

Chase's mouth fell open.

Dylan Lynn Cott and his mother had both come to the Path to Eden, the latter with a history of substance abuse. Dylan then went on to molest Ali Rennick, Elijah Kane's right-hand man's daughter. He'd ended up dead and his mother was convinced that the Path to Eden, and probably Trent Bain, had something to do with it.

What the fuck?

"Linus, did you ever find out which officer arrested Dylan? And who signed the death certificate?"

"I did. And they were one and the same. Trent Bain."

"Fuck."

Despite all the evidence pointing in his direction, Chase didn't want to believe that Trent was actually part of this deadly scheme.

Even though the Duffy Group case had been closed more than four years ago, the idea that the very people who had taken an oath to protect the public were endangering them still stung.

"I've got a cell phone coming your way."

"Another one?" Linus asked.

"Another one. I need to know what's on it."

"Well, if it's anything like the one belonging to Bob what's-his-name, then I suspect… nothing."

"Just look. Can you also do a background check on Derek Rennick?"

"Sure thing. I'll get back to you—"

"Like, now?"

"Of course."

"Like before, I'm going to mute this side of the conversation. Just holler when you find something."

Tate and Chase left Elijah Kane's room in a hurry.

Downstairs they found Dr. Mason speaking to Dr. Niccolo.

"Dr. Mason," Chase said quickly, "do you have a list of names of everyone who has given blood samples? Everyone who lives at the Path to Eden?"

"Of course," he said. "We require their name in order to match their result with their sample."

"You have this on a computer?"

Dr. Mason nodded.

"I do. Just over here."

They moved away from Dr. Niccolo and followed Dr. Mason into an adjacent wing. Chase was impressed by the setup, especially considering that Dr. Mason had called it a 'small-scale operation'.

A series of privacy tents had been erected and she counted at least four nurses collecting samples from members of the Path to Eden. Space-age medical equipment covered nearly every square inch of counter space.

Noticing her gaze, Dr. Mason said, "We can only do some rudimentary testing here, most of it has to be shipped back to the lab for proper RT-PCR testing."

Chase wasn't interested in the samples; not now, anyway.

"Where's the computer?"

Dr. Mason indicated a laptop sitting on a desk.

"I want you to search for a name—Derek Rennick."

Dr. Mason's fingers flashed across the keys.

"We have a Reynolds, Daisy, and a Rendell, Thomas, but no Rennick."

Chase whipped her head around to stare at Tate.

"Shit, he's not here," she said. "Derek Rennick isn't here."

Chapter 33

"**HAS ANYBODY SEEN DEREK? DEREK** Rennick?" Chase hollered at the crowd of people who were silently praying in the church.

A smattering of head shakes interspersed with a few verbal 'nos'.

"Anyone?" she asked desperately.

More negative responses.

"God dammit, where is he?" Chase walked over to the first person she saw, a woman who was on her knees, tears in her eyes, and grasped her shoulder.

"Have you seen Derek Rennick?"

The woman was shocked, but she managed to shake her head.

"I haven't seen him since before the night… the night that Elijah was attacked."

Chase approached another woman who was watering a plant that hung from one of the church's wooden walls.

"What about you? Have you seen Derek?"

"No, he wasn't here last night."

Chase scratched her head.

"Why were you here? Why did you gather?"

"Derek said that Elijah had something important to tell us."

Chase cringed. This woman—all of these people—had no idea just how close they'd come to being infected.

She shook these feelings away.

"But he's always by Elijah's side, right?"

"Usually. But he wasn't last night."

"Shit," Chase said.

This wasn't making sense. Typically, leaders of a cult surrounded themselves with 'yes men', people who agreed with them no matter how extreme their views inevitably became.

Where was Derek Rennick?

In Elijah's absence, he was slated to take over.

So, where was he?

With Tate in tow, Chase hastened out of the church and approached Marshall Woods.

"Get your people to start asking around about Derek Rennick."

"Who?"

"Derek Rennick. Should be hard to miss, long gray hair, young face." She thrust the voice changer and cell phone at him. "And get these to Quantico, *ASAP*."

Chase could tell that he had more questions, but Marshall was a man of action. He immediately gathered his troops and started pointing and giving orders.

The immediacy of Marshall's behavior was appreciated. Often, contemplation hindered execution, especially when it came to law enforcement.

"Chase? You there?" Linus said. "Chase, take me off mute, I found something. I found—"

Chase unmuted her phone.

"Go."

"You're not gonna believe this, but the Path to Eden used to be called something different."

"What do you mean?"

"I found some old tax documents from about twelve years ago, it looks like Derek Rennick set up his own religious-affiliated thingy. It was called the Path of Enlightenment, but I can't find anything about them online."

"That's probably because they have the same tenets as the Path to Eden and shun technology," Chase muttered.

"Maybe. But you not gonna believe what happened to the Path of Enlightenment." Linus was so excited that he seemed out of breath.

"Come on, just spit it out."

"Well, they started on the same plot of land—that's how I found the connection—which was gifted to them by the LDS. Apparently, it was just a small movement back then, this Path of Enlightenment, and Derek Rennick was listed as the only officer. I cross-referenced his name with death reports, and I discovered that he had four daughters—not just Ali. Two of them are dead. Want to take a stab at how they died?"

Chase hated guessing games, she hated the way that Linus took his time revealing them important information. But in this case, she felt compelled to answer.

"Measles."

"Yeah, measles. Two of his daughters, Jesse and Jamie, died from *measles*."

"Holy fuck," Tate muttered. "He's the one behind this. He recruited Elijah Kane."

Chase could barely nod—the pieces were falling into place now and they seemed to physically impact her brain.

Derek Rennick tried to start his own cult, the Path of Enlightenment, and only had a few members when measles ravaged the community, killing two of his daughters.

Chase pictured the man's flat affect and his monotone way of speaking.

Derek realized that he couldn't do this on his own. If he wanted to start again, if he wanted to grow, he needed a figurehead. Someone charismatic, someone with a soothing voice, someone who had the ability to command a crowd.

Someone like Elijah Kane.

Elijah was the figurehead, but Derek was the one pulling the strings.

"That's the reason no one's leaving," Tate remarked huskily. "They must know that Derek is *really* the one in charge.

"Chase—"

"Gotta go, thanks, Linus."

She hung up.

"Trent Bain told his brother that we were going to storm the castle," Chase said, "And as Elijah's right-hand man, Derek caught wind of this and took off. Tate, he took off with the virus."

Tate swallowed hard.

"The virus… and the *kids*."

Chase pulled her gun free, and she stared off into the distance. A mile away, maybe further, something metal reflected the sun's powerful rays.

"You're right, and I think I know where he's hiding."

Chapter 34

CHASE'S THEORY THAT DEREK RENNICK had set up shop in the abandoned Tyson Foods building at the boundary of the Path to Eden's property was immediately confirmed by the sight of an 18-wheeler idling on the cracked asphalt.

Moving quickly with their guns drawn, Chase and Tate approached the truck. The keys were in the ignition and thick black smoke spewed from the rusted tailpipe, but the cab was empty. The trailer doors hung open and, thankfully, this was unoccupied as well.

They weren't too late to stop this.

Most of the front of the rundown building was comprised of a loading dock. Chase suspected this was where Michael Lawson had backed the truck into to load the kids on board.

The garage door was askew, permanently so, it appeared, but even at its widest point, it was only open about six or eight inches. Not wide enough for the sun to reveal anything but shadows within and definitely not gaping enough for her to slide beneath it.

To the left was another door, this of the regular variety, but it was firmly closed.

Chase indicated with two fingers for Tate to go around back, to find an alternative entrance, but he vehemently shook his head.

She scowled, hoping that he could pick up her displeasure through the mask that they both still sported on their faces.

"Go around back," she ordered.

Tate continued to resist.

"We should wait—wait for SWAT."

Except they hadn't told SWAT or anyone else where they were going. Marshall Woods was off scouring the compound for Derek Rennick, and he was about the only person Chase thought she could trust. She didn't know how far Trent Bain and by extension, Elijah Kane's influence had infiltrated the MBI or the Billings police force.

And by letting them know, they risked tipping Derek off.

Again.

"We have to act now," she said. "Tate, we have to act, *right now.*"

Tate screwed up his face, which was accentuated by the thick plastic covering his features.

Chase aggressively pointed down the side of the building. The truck backfired, making them both jump.

"Go!" she hissed.

Tate finally relented. Chase waited for her partner to disappear from sight before silently approaching the loading bay door.

Once there, she waited.

The sound of faint voices encouraged her to move closer still. When Chase still had difficulty determining what was being said, she lowered herself and peered through the opening.

Shadows… shadows of children's feet.

"You are gonna do great things as ambassadors for the Path to Eden. I know it's hard to leave all this behind, but when you return, you will be welcomed as heroes."

Chase recognized Derek Rennick's flat voice.

"But—but Elijah's dead," a small boy spoke up.

"Elijah's *not* dead. That's just what they want you to think. All those people out there, all those cops, hate us for what we represent. They're addicted to their cell phones, they think that it makes them smarter than us, better than us, but it doesn't. And if anybody tries to—"

"But the blood... I saw the blood."

"Fake," Derek Rennick assured the child. "It's all fake. What this world needs is a cleansing. And with the skills you acquire at our sister institution, you will bring us the tools we need not just to survive, but to *thrive*."

The speech was clichéd, and Derek's voice cracked several times during the delivery.

No wonder he needed someone like Elijah Kane, Chase thought.

She spotted several of the feet shifting awkwardly, but there were no further protests.

"Good. Now, it's going to be a long trip and I won't lie to you; it won't be easy. But I've prepared some medicine to help you get through it."

Chase knew she had to do something fast. She pulled herself off the ground and scampered to the door next to the garage.

She aimed her gun, then noticed that the handle had already been dented and hung loosely from its housing.

It was unlocked.

Chase took a deep breath, adjusted her grip on her pistol, then pulled the door open.

"Derek Rennick put your hands in the air," she shouted.

Chase took one step into the warehouse and was immediately struck completely blind.

Chapter 35

It was the sun—Chase hadn't accounted for the sun.

Even with the mask covering her eyes, moving from the bright Montana daylight to the dark interior of the abandoned warehouse messed with her eyes.

She couldn't see anything.

Chase did, however, have a singular thought: *We should have waited for the SWAT.*

"FBI—Derek Rennick, hands in the air," she yelled blindly.

There was a flicker of movement and Chase heard shuffling feet.

She swung the gun in that direction.

"Don't move! Don't *fucking* move!"

Nobody listened—the shuffling continued.

"Put the gun down and take off your mask," Derek said.

Chase's eyes were starting to adjust now, but not quickly enough.

"I'm the one with a gun," she said, taking a chance that Derek shunned weapons the way he shunned cell phones. "You do as I say, or I'll put a bullet between your eyes."

She heard several people suck air into their lungs—the kids, it had to be the kids.

"I don't have a gun, but what I have in my hand is far more dangerous."

Chase blinked and was finally able to see.

Most of the children—at least a dozen of them—had backed away and were pressed up against the interior walls of the warehouse.

All but one.

Derek had wrapped an arm around a child and was holding him close to his chest. In his other hand, he held a vial of clear liquid.

He had a sinister smile on his face.

"Remove the mask and drop the gun," Derek repeated. He blew a strand of gray hair from in front of his face.

"It's over, Derek. I know what happened to your daughters. I know what happened to Jesse and Jamie."

Derek's expression didn't falter.

"You know nothing. You know nothing about this world."

"Your shitty parables and canned lines aren't gonna work on me."

The man laughed. The sound was full of mirth.

"You're part of the problem. You and that drone of yours, taking pictures, sending them online, spamming, liking, subscribing—*you're* the problem. This world needs to be cleansed of people like you."

"By using *them*?" Chase said, taking aim with her gun and nodding at the children. "They're the problem, too?"

Another laugh.

"No, they're not the problem. They're the *solution*."

Chase hated the way that Derek made his ridiculous claims sound as if they had merit. He might not be charismatic, but he was a true believer, and that carried weight. One of the kids actually started to nod in agreement.

It was time to put an end to this demented fantasy.

"The *solution*? You're going to sacrifice these children to some virus because you believe that they're part of the solution?"

"I'm not sacrificing anyone," Derek said coldly. "God will decide—God will decide if they live or die, not me."

"Like God chose for Jamie and Jesse to die? Like God decided that Dylan Lynn Cott should target your youngest daughter?"

The greasy smile finally disappeared.

"I'll ask you one more time, take off your mask and lower your gun. I'll give you to the count of three and if you don't listen, I'll break this vial and infect everybody in here."

Chase needed to stall long enough for Tate to find a way in.

"One… two…"

Before Derek could utter the word 'three' Chase sucked in a huge breath. Then she peeled off her mask and set both it and her gun on the concrete floor.

"Take me," she offered, showing the man her empty palms. "Let these kids go and take me instead."

Derek was surprised by her obedience.

"Good… *good*. Now, how much time do I have before the others show up?"

There are no others, Chase thought. *Except for Tate. Where are you, Tate?*

She ignored the man's query.

"I know all about you, Derek Rennick. I know about how you tried to form your own cult, and how you couldn't do it, how you needed someone like Elijah Kane."

Derek's eyes narrowed.

"Elijah Kane is a simple man obsessed with sex. He doesn't care about the cause, not really. He hasn't been through the things I've been through. He doesn't believe in the cleanse."

"I know, I know," Chase placated. "But do these kids believe?" She allowed her eyes to drift to all of their frightened faces. "They're just kids. They're not true believers."

Derek shook his head.

"It doesn't matter."

"What doesn't matter is that virus," Chase countered. "We're already working on a vaccine. In a few hours, that thing you have in your hand will be as dangerous as the common cold."

It was a bald-faced lie. Chase just hoped that Trent hadn't told his half-brother that nobody had so much as mentioned a potential vaccine.

"*Ha!* Technology? Everyone thinks that technology will save them, but it couldn't save my girls. And this virus," he marveled at the clear liquid, "is a testament to that."

"*You* could have saved your girls," Chase stated, knowing that she was treading on thin ice. "All you had to do was give them the vaccine. But you refused—*why*? Because it wasn't part of your belief system?"

"It couldn't save them!" Derek yelled. He tightened his grip on the boy's throat, and she saw all the muscles in his thin neck contract. "Technology couldn't save them—nothing could!"

"You mean, *you* couldn't save them. Let them go, Derek."

"These children are ambassadors, spreading the new wave. When people realize that their medicine and all of their fancy machines can't save them, they'll have no choice but to adopt our way of living. They'll have no choice but to follow the Path to Eden."

Chase suppressed a laugh.

"All this from a little virus?"

Derek tilted the vial.

"Not just a—"

"A virus that was made in a lab," Chase interjected. "A virus that you used technology to genetically modify. Don't you see the irony here?"

Oh, he saw it, all right, but Derek was too far gone to understand the implications.

"Sometimes you must become the devil to beat him at his own game."

"Who made the virus, Derek?" Chase demanded.

The man cocked his head.

"Ah, so you don't know everything. You know about Jamie and Jesse and Ali, you know about the Path of Enlightenment, but you don't know who made the virus?"

"No, I—"

Everything happened so fast that Chase didn't get a chance to react.

Tate lunged from the shadows, driving his shoulder into Derek's spine.

"No!" she screamed. "No, Tate don't do it! He has the virus!"

But it was too late, and the three of them, Derek, Tate, and the child fell forward, crashing into a heap on the ground. Despite all of these sounds their bodies made, including at least one shout from one of the other kids, Chase heard a singular noise, loud and clear: breaking glass.

Chapter 36

CHASE ACTED QUICKLY, SCOOPING HER mask off the floor and sprinting across the warehouse toward the pile of people.

Tired as he was, Tate had no problem subduing the much older and overweight man.

"Get out!" she screamed at everyone. *"Get out!"*

The kids were confused, unsure of what to do, didn't move.

"Run!"

Now they dispersed, some diving and sliding beneath the bay door while others exited the way that Chase had entered.

She reached the boy first and flipped him onto his back. Then she slid her mask over his face.

"You, too. Just keep the mask on and get out of here."

The boy, seemingly unhurt, scampered to his feet and sprinted away.

Tate rolled Derek over as Chase pulled the collar of her shirt over her nose and mouth.

As he cuffed the man, her partner used his knee to grind Derek's face into the concrete.

"Chase, you don't have a mask," Tate said, his eyes wild. "You need to get—"

Chase didn't hear the end of his sentence. As she reached out to search Derek's pockets, she accidentally brushed against the bare skin of his arm.

And for the second time since entering the Tyson Foods warehouse, Chase went blind.

***

"What do you mean, you can't do anything for them?" Derek begged. "They're sick! Look at them!"

He couldn't take his gaze off his two girls. Jessie was in worse shape than Jamie. Her eyes fluttered ever so slightly, and her skin was a bright red. Jamie was faring better, but she had the spots; a series of painful red bumps covered nearly every square inch of her face. Sweat dampened both of their beautiful heads of hair.

"Daddy?" Jamie said. The agony in her voice broke his heart.

"Look at them!" he screamed.

"Mr. Rennick, we are doing everything we can. We've managed to lower their fever, but the virus… it has spread. The only thing that we can do for them now is keep them comfortable."

Derek's eyes bulged and he grabbed the skinny doctor by the throat.

"Save my girls," he hissed. "You save my fucking *girls!"*

Derek began squeezing the man's throat, cutting off his air supply. Instead of trying to fend him off, the doctor frantically gestured with his arms.

"Save them!"

Thick hands grasped Derek's shoulders and pulled. But he rooted himself to the floor.

"Save… them…"

Two more hands grabbed him and when they yanked, Derek had no choice but to finally let go of the doctor.

The man immediately broke into a coughing fit and massaged his throat.

"You have to save *them!" Derek screamed as he was roughly drawn backward.*

"Mr. Rennick, calm down," a voice said in his ear.

Derek bucked.

"All this fucking technology and you can't do anything!" Spit flew from his lips. "What good is it? What good is technology if it doesn't fucking work!*"*

"Calm down," the voice instructed again.

The doctor, finally having regained his faculties, glared at him.

*"*You *could have saved them," he said hoarsely. "All you had to was get them vaccinated. Don't you dare put this on me."*

The doctor's words inspired new rage in Derek, and he redoubled his efforts. But the nurses or security guards or whoever was holding him was ready for this outburst.

He failed to break loose.

*"Fuck you!" Derek kicked the air. "*Fuck you!*"*

He was dragged to a separate room, away from his daughters who were in quarantine.

"Daddy?" It wasn't Jamie this time, but Ali.

Seeing her cherubic face finally inspired calm and sensing this change, he was finally released.

How did she not get sick? *Derek wondered.* How is this… how is this *possible?*

"Stay calm, Mr. Rennick, or I'll be forced to call the police."

It was a nurse, he saw—a male nurse with massive arms and a muscular chest.

"Save them," was all Derek could muster. A weak, pathetic plea.

"I'm sorry."

Derek, crying now, grabbed Ali and held her close.

"Are they going to die, Daddy? Are Jamie and Jessie going to die?"

Derek looked up and saw his eldest daughter, her blond hair a mess on top of her head.

He couldn't bring himself to answer.

All he could do was weep.

The Path to Enlightenment might be dead, but another would form in its place, Derek vowed. Bigger, better.

And when it did, he would act.

Derek Rennick would avenge his daughter's death and make all those who revered the false God that was technology pay.

***

"—out of here!"

Chase gasped as she retracted her hand and, avoiding the liquid that had spilled on the ground, made sure she didn't touch Derek as she continued to search for weapons or more vials.

She found neither but did retrieve his wallet.

"Chase, you don't have a mask, you need to get out of here!"

She tore into the wallet.

There was Derek's ID and some cash—evidently, cash *wasn't* evil—but what held her interest was the folded photograph she found tucked into one of the smaller pockets.

It was worn and faded, and she had to unfold carefully for fear of it breaking apart in her hands.

Chase saw a younger version of Derek Rennick, smiling, his hands around two young girls, most likely Jesse and Jamie. In front of them, on her knees with her chin propped up in her hands, her lower half buried in sand, was Ali.

And then there was the fourth daughter.

Chase squinted at the image.

Jesse and Jamie had died from measles infection, but Ali had survived only to be molested later by Dylan Lynn Cott.

But the fourth child…

Unlike the others, this girl was a little older than the rest, and she had blond hair.

"Chase, please! You need to get out of here! You don't have a mask."

She was so transfixed by what she saw that Chase didn't even hear her partner's words.

The girl in the photo was a good fifteen years younger, but her plain face still inspired recognition. With a trembling hand, Chase turned the photo around and showed it to Tate.

"Who does that look like to you?"

"Chase, please," Tate begged. "You need—"

"Just *look!* Who does that look like to you?"

Derek tried to lift his head in response to her request, but Tate shoved it hard against the floor. Chase heard the man's teeth click off the hard surface.

"I don't—holy shit," Tate breathed. "That's Helen, isn't it? It's Helen Niccolo."

Derek started to laugh.

"Shut up!" Chase cried. "Shut the fuck up!"

Derek stopped chuckling, but he did not go quiet.

Instead, the man said in his monotone voice, "Let the soil beneath our feet remind us of our origins and the path we must follow. To Eden, we return, to Eden, we belong."

Chapter 37

"**WE HAVE TO GET YOU** to a hospital and into quarantine. We need to stop the virus before it spreads," Tate said desperately.

Chase took the mask that Marshall Woods gave her outside the warehouse and slipped it on, double and then triple-checking to make sure that the buckles were securely fastened.

The entire warehouse was a quarantine zone now, and Dr. Mason was busy taking buccal swabs and blood samples from the children, who looked absolutely shell-shocked by what had just happened. Thankfully, Dr. Mason suggested that it was unlikely at the distance they'd been from the vial when it had broken that they were infected.

Even the kid, Thomas Brewer, whom Derek Rennick had accosted, was likely safe. And for a man who prided himself on not making any guesses and only spouted cold hard facts, this hypothesis from Dr. Mason was good enough for her.

With Chase, he waffled. She was probably, maybe, most likely okay.

Also, good enough for her.

As for Derek, he had a mask on now, too. Only, Chase had made sure that she applied liberal amounts of Dr. Mason's surgical tape to securely shut his lips before someone covered his face.

"Later," she replied to Tate.

"Later? No, *now*. We need to get you checked out; we need to make sure—"

"I have a mask on, Tate. If I'm infected, I won't spread it to anybody else. Dr. Mason assured me of that. We have to find Helen Niccolo."

"She took off," Marshall informed them both. He seemed particularly disgruntled, and Chase wasn't sure if this was because he felt guilty for just letting the woman walk away or if he was pissed because they'd left him out of their plan. "After you started asking about Derek Rennick in the church, I saw her slink off. Left in her car. If I had known she was involved in this somehow, I would never have let her go."

It wasn't the mustachioed man's fault. If anything, it was Chase's fault.

She'd been so distracted by how much of an asshole Trent Bain was that she just assumed that he was responsible for feeding information about the case to his half-brother. All the while, it had been Dr. Niccolo.

Dr. Niccolo who had been called in as a specialist to offer insight into the infection had somehow managed to weasel herself into nearly every aspect of their investigation. Niccolo, who had engineered the virus to make it more deadly.

Chase couldn't believe she missed it.

Who else could have possibly made the virus?

Elijah Kane with his communications degree? Or maybe Derek Rennick who had barely graduated high school?

Chase bit her lip as penance.

"I've got an APB out on Dr. Niccolo's car," Marshall said.

Chase considered this.

Would Niccolo run?

Unlikely. She must have known that they'd find her father Derek and when they did, the gig would be up.

And what does a cornered rat do?

It fights tooth and nail.

"Where's her lab?" Chase asked.

Marshall held her gaze.

"She works out of Niccolo Pharmaceutical."

Chase winced. She'd been hoping that Niccolo ran a small laboratory, thus limiting her access to equipment and resources. But the name Niccolo Pharmaceutical brought to mind a large-scale operation.

One that could easily pivot to spread the virus by contaminating whatever medicine they manufactured or distributed.

That's where Niccolo would go.

A cornered rat would fight, but if there was a chance to return to their burrow where they felt comfortable, they would do that first.

"She's going back to her lab," Chase said with confidence.

Marshall nodded in agreement.

"I'll go," he offered. "I'll go with Agent Abernathy."

"No, stay here—I'm going with Tate."

"Chase, that's not a good idea. You could be infected. Every minute we wait is more time for the virus to replicate in your lungs. You heard Dr. Mason; your best chance at survival is large doses of antiretrovirals. The sooner the better."

Chase hated the look on Tate's face, the pitiful, hopeless expression.

"I don't care, I—"

"Do you remember those kids?" Tate said frantically. "Remember how they looked? How their brains basically swelled and exploded inside their heads, Chase? You remember Bob Santelli? You want that to happen to you?"

Chase ignored the pain in her partner's voice.

The truth was, she *didn't* care. What she cared about were the six kids who had died because of a group of demented and vindictive individuals.

What she cared about were the countless other children who might become infected if Niccolo spread the virus.

"Chase, I'm not going to budge on this, okay?" Tate said, his entire body stiffening. "If you don't go with Dr. Mason right now—"

"You'll what?" Chase challenged, feeling her temperature rise. Sweat immediately beaded on her forehead. "What are you going to do, Tate?"

Tate lowered his eyes, which Chase interpreted as him acquiescing. She'd seen that look countless times before when Tate had tried to protect her during the course of duty. Hell, Chase had seen it mere minutes ago when she'd instructed him to head down the side of the warehouse to find an alternative way in.

But this time, her read was dead wrong.

"Arrest her," Tate said softly.

The comment was directed at Marshall Woods, but the man didn't react.

"Arrest me?" Chase scoffed. "Tate—"

"Chase, if you're not willing to go with Dr. Mason right now, Marshall Woods is going to arrest you."

"You wouldn't," she said. Chase tried to minimize the hurt she felt from creeping into her voice, but she did a poor job keeping it at bay.

"Agent Woods," Tate said, raising his voice, "I'm heading up this case, I'm the senior Agent, and I am ordering you to arrest Agent Chase Adams."

Marshall Woods' eyes widened, then narrowed. Unbelievably, the man reached for the cuffs looped on his hip.

"I'm sorry," he said.

Chase debated her options. She could run, but *where*? It's not like she would get far—there were dozens of cops surrounding the warehouse, and that said nothing of the SWAT team, the EMTs, and every law enforcement agency acronym she could think of. Even if she got away, then what? Every moment Tate wasted looking for her was more time that Dr. Niccolo had to finish what her father had started.

Reluctantly, Chase turned around and put her hands behind her back. She glared at Tate while Marshall loosely applied the handcuffs.

"Sorry," Marshall repeated to which, Chase said nothing. Again, it wasn't his fault.

But this time it wasn't hers either.

It was Tate's.

As much as she wanted to keep her mouth shut, as much as she knew that she would undoubtedly regret anything she said now, Chase was helpless to prevent herself from speaking.

It was just who she was.

When someone got in her way, no matter if they loved her or loathed her, Chase had only one reaction: to hurt them.

Hurt them as badly as she could.

"You want to know why we never got married, Tate?"

"Chase, please. I'm doing—"

"Because of this," Chase spat. "Because you won't let me do my *fucking* job. Because your personal relationships trump everything else. But for me? For me, this job means *everything*. You're weak and that's why I won't marry you."

"I'm sorry."

This time it wasn't SWAT agent Marshall Woods who said the words but her partner and fiancé, Tate Abernathy.

Chapter 38

TATE RACED ACROSS THE CITY with Marshall Woods in the passenger seat beside him. The man was tough, he knew that much. A tough man who seemed principled, which Tate admired.

He was also scared shitless by Tate's driving.

Tate often wondered why he drove the way did, and Chase had asked him about it on several occasions.

He didn't really have an answer.

Maybe it was because he was testing fate, thinking that perhaps if he got into an accident then it would somehow put him on equal footing with his wife and daughter.

It could be simpler than that. Maybe he just liked going fast.

But Tate was aware that he was traveling too quickly, even for him—the lights of the squad cars that followed them to Niccolo Pharmaceutical faded in the rearview.

"Jesus Christ, slow down," Marshall said through gritted teeth.

Tate ignored him. If anything, he pushed the rental even harder.

He was still grappling with the events at the Tyson Foods warehouse.

What other choice did he have other than to have Chase detained?

It was for her safety—for all of *their* safety.

But that look in Chase's eyes…

Tate had come across men with evil stares, horrible men, despicable individuals. But he didn't think a single one of them had ever looked at him the way Chase Adams just had.

The GPS announced their impending arrival around the same time Tate spotted the building.

The modest two-story structure was constructed completely of glass, but the way the now-setting sun glinted off the sides gave it an almost celestial appearance.

The real Path to Eden is through Niccolo Pharma, he thought ironically.

"I've been here before," Marshall said.

Tate raised an eyebrow, but the man shrugged this off.

"Unrelated case. All the trucks are around back. We should go there first, make sure we stop any outgoing shipments."

Tate was struck by how different Marshall's approach was compared to Chase.

Chase would have sacrificed everything and everyone to get Helen Niccolo.

There was no denying that she was a selfish person. But he didn't blame her. Chase was confused, frequently mistaking self-interest for altruism.

And why? Because of something that happened to her as a child? Something that she had no control over?

Is she ever going to forgive herself for leaving her sister with the Jalston brothers?

"Around back it is," Tate said and then yanked the wheel so hard to the left that two of the car's tires lifted off the ground. When they jumped the curb Marshall's head smacked the ceiling and he cried out.

For a moment, when it appeared as if they were going to collide headlong with a massive semi-truck, a vision flashed before Tate's eyes.

He saw his daughter's face, snowball white, as the headlights of an oncoming car blinded her. She tried to turn, but the rain-slicked road offered no traction.

Someone screamed—*Rachel? Robyn?*—and the—

"Tate!" Marshall shouted, bringing Tate back to the present.

He cranked the steering wheel in the opposite direction and managed to avert disaster.

The semi honked and the rear of their car smashed into the front bumper, sending the much smaller vehicle spinning.

Before it came to a full stop, Tate jumped out, gun drawn.

"What the fuck do you think you're doing?"

Tate pointed his weapon at the fat man standing half-in and half-out of his truck.

"Billings SWAT, hands in the air!" It was Marshall doing the yelling this time.

Two meaty palms rocketed to the sky.

"What the fuck is going on?" the driver demanded.

"A little late for deliveries, isn't it?" Tate asked, eying the man up.

Was this just an innocent bystander or another Michael Lawson or Bob Santilli? Had this man also been indoctrinated by the Path to Eden?

He had no way of knowing.

"Hey—hey, I'm just a delivery guy. Boss offered to pay double to get these pills out tonight," the man protested.

"Keep your hands in the air and step down from the truck. Turn around and walk slowly toward us," Marshall said.

"Just don't fucking shoot, alright? It's only meds in the truck, nothing you can get high on. I don't know what you expect—" Tate took aim. "Take it—I don't give a fuck. Take all of it."

The driver jumped to the ground and started to follow Marshall's instructions.

"Over there, on the grass. Get on your knees."

"Is she in there?" Tate asked. The night sky had blossomed with red and blue lights, combining to form an eerie purple reminiscent of the Aurora Borealis.

"Who?"

"Dr. Niccolo," Tate shouted impatiently. "Is Dr. Niccolo inside?"

"Yeah, I think she's in the labs. Are you going to—"

With his free hand, Marshall reached out and gave the man a hard shove in the back. Not forceful enough to send to the ground, but enough that he lost his balance.

"I'm going in, Marshall. Wait for everyone else to get here, then follow me."

"You can't wait?"

Tate glanced at the truck. It was a massive vehicle, perhaps even bigger than the one that they'd found the kids in. And that truck had easily held six bodies. Tate could only imagine how many small vials of the virus mixed in with whatever pharmaceuticals that Niccolo Pharma distributed could fit in the back.

Millions? *Tens* of millions?

"No, I'm going in now."

Tate adjusted his mask, which had come loose during the accident, and sprinted toward the open loading dock. He put his gun away just long enough to hoist himself up and silently thanked Chase for making him do all that stupid running—running he hated.

Tate pulled his gun out once more and found himself in an area filled with skids of drugs that nearly reached the twenty-foot ceiling.

He briefly glanced at the unlabeled white containers and wondered how many of these were contaminated.

Then he thought about what they would do with this place.

Burn it to the ground, Tate thought. *I hope they burn the whole fucking place to the ground.*

Tate continued deeper into the dark warehouse until he came to a door marked employees only. He tried to force it open but found it locked. Tate hammered the butt of his pistol on the window.

"Open the door!" he yelled. "Open the *fucking* door!"

A portly man wearing an all-blue uniform and a ridiculous hat—a combination of an English Bobby and an NYPD cop—appeared.

The man saw the gun and he revealed the whites of his eyes. Tate wasn't sure if his voice could be heard through the thick pane of glass, so he pressed his badge up against the window as he hollered, "FBI—I need you to let me in, right now!"

The man used a key on his belt to unlock the door and the second Tate heard the lock disengage, he shoved the door open. It struck the security guard in the hip, and he twisted to the ground in pain.

"Where's Dr. Niccolo?"

The security guard's reaction was similar to that of the truck driver: bewilderment.

"What the hell is—"

"Where is Dr. Niccolo?" Tate didn't exactly point his gun at the man but didn't exactly lower it, either.

"She—she's in the labs."

"Where the fuck are the labs?"

The man pointed behind him and then hooked his fingers to the right.

"Down the hall, around the first bend."

The man once again asked what was going on, but Tate was already gone. He silently thanked God for the security guard because, without him, Tate doubted he would have ever found the labs. Every hallway and room looked the same: aseptic with identical bleached walls. Alien-looking equipment inside fume hoods. Thick-paned windows.

After passing through a set of flapping doors Tate was confronted by a large sign overhead: a yellow biohazard symbol and a reminder not to enter without proper protective equipment. Tate busted through these doors, too, and found himself in a sort of anteroom the circumference of which was covered in a series of lockers indicating which type of safety gear was contained inside. The true biohazard room was in front of him, a rectangular space that was flanked by a wall of windows.

There was only one door into this space, but it didn't look like something that Tate could either break or shoot his way through.

The text on the door, in big, block letters, confirmed his suspicions.

WARNING: THIS ROOM IS UNDER NEGATIVE PRESSURE. WHEN OCCUPIED IT CAN **ONLY** BE OPENED FROM THE INSIDE.

And there was someone inside.

Dr. Helen Niccolo was wearing a lab coat, and her blond hair was pulled up into a messy bun. She was holding a pipette in one hand and was in the process of injecting liquid into a familiar-looking vial.

"Niccolo," Tate shouted. The thick glass muffled the sound, but his voice was loud enough for the entire building to hear.

Dr. Niccolo, startled by the noise, looked up.

"Or should I call you Dr. Rennick?"

Something flashed over Dr. Niccolo's face.

Apathy? Complacency? Boredom?

"You're too late, Agent Abernathy," the woman said hoarsely. "You're *too* late. The truck already left, and in an hour the contaminated vials will be stocked in dozens of pharmacies all across the Midwest. Thank God for twenty-four-hour service. By morning, my measles virus will have spread like wildfire."

Dr. Niccolo had no idea that they'd stopped the truck.

Tate intended to keep it that way.

"Is this what your sisters would've wanted? You think Jesse and Jamie would be proud?" Tate asked, taking a play out of Chase's handbook.

The woman threw her head back and laughed.

"What *they* want? Really? Tate, what my sisters want is irrelevant. It's what God wants that matters."

"And God wants *this*?"

Dr. Niccolo looked at him as if she were trying to explain calculus to an ant.

"Of course. Why do you think he spared me?"

Maybe Tate was an ant because he was having a hard time following.

Recognizing this, Dr. Niccolo sighed.

"He took Jessie and Jamie but left me and Ali and my father because we had a greater purpose to fulfill." Niccolo tilted the pipette. "And this is that purpose."

"It's a fucking virus, Helen. You said so yourself: its purpose is to infect, to reprogram, and destroy the host. That's it. It's not a tool for… for spiritual purification."

"That's where you're wrong. God made this virus like he made everything around us. It's the ultimate selection tool. But man fucked it up." With every word that came out of her mouth, Helen Niccolo's eyes became progressively more frantic. "They made vaccines and ruined His plan. But this—this can't be stopped."

Tate knew that he would get nowhere by challenging the woman's religious dogma, so he changed tactics and attempted to use her own words against her.

"So, you modified His plan? You? A mere mortal? And kids? Really, Helen? You're using kids to spread this disease?"

"That was my father's idea. He thought it would be poetic, seeing as God took Jesse and Jamie while they were so young. I tried to convince him to unleash the virus last night when he got that simpleton Elijah to gather everyone in the church. But he didn't want to."

Oh, yeah, Derek's a real fucking Walt Whitman, Tate thought, recalling what he'd overheard the man telling the kids back in the warehouse. Some shit about them being ambassadors.

More like harbingers of death.

Tate's eyes dropped to the necklace that dangled in front of Niccolo' lab coat. Two diamonds—he remembered when they'd first met, and Chase had helped her untangle them from her mask.

Two diamonds, two dead sisters.

"But this is my idea. It's much simpler and more effective. But you wouldn't understand because you are still married to this idea that technology makes us better. It doesn't—it's an affront to Him and everything He stands for."

Tate broke character and laughed; he couldn't help it.

"You're holding a fucking pipette in your hand." Tate indicated the room in which he was standing. "And this entire building was built on technology. *Your* building. Goddamn it, it even has your name on it: *Niccolo Pharmaceuticals*."

He expected his comment, which should have made her realize the irony of their situation, to enrage the woman but she had a response for this, too.

"I gave myself that name, *Niccolo*. You want to know how I came up with it?"

"I want to know what you plan on doing with that vial."

Dr. Niccolo ignored him.

"I got it from Niccolo Machiavelli, the famous Italy ruler who believed that the ends justified the means. And that, Tate, is what this is. Sometimes… sometimes you must become the devil to beat him at his own game."

There he was again, Derrick 'Robert Frost' Rennick—Dr. Niccolo's father had uttered these exact words back in the warehouse.

"An end to *what*?"

"This world, you *plebe*. Don't you see? The world we live in is pure filth. We turned His beautiful creation into a steaming pile of garbage. Pornography is rampant, there are underage girls starting Only Fans pages, influencers literally killing each other for a like and views. It's disgusting. That's why I created this virus. God will decide who lives and who dies, just like He wanted."

Tate had about enough of this. He raised his gun and aimed through the window at Dr. Niccolo's head.

"Open the door, Dr. Niccolo. Open it, *now*."

"Or what? You'll shoot? The joke's on you—this is bulletproof glass."

And now you're standing behind the very technology you so despise.

"Only the worthy survive, is that right?"

"Now, you're catching on."

"Like your father?" Dr. Niccolo's brow knitted, and Tate nodded. "Yeah, that's right. We caught him before he could infect any more children. And he was exposed, Niccolo."

"You're lying," she hissed.

"I'm not—how do you think I found you?"

Niccolo seemed to contemplate this for several moments before, like his previous comment, she merely dismissed this question.

"It doesn't matter—if God wills it, it will be."

Tate tightened his grip on the gun.

"Open the fucking door."

"I told you—" Tate didn't think, he just acted. He aimed just to the left of Helen Niccolo and pulled the trigger three times. The sound was even louder here than in the church, which had been designed to amplify noise, and his ears immediately started to ring.

Niccolo didn't even move. True to her word, the glass was bulletproof. There were three indentations in the glass surrounded by a spiderweb of cracks, but the bullets fell harmlessly to the ground.

Barely audible over the persistent tinnitus in his ears, Tate heard someone approaching from behind.

It was Marshall Woods.

"God dammit."

"The doors are locked, I can't get in," he told the masked SWAT agent. "Get a battering ram, let's break this fucking thing down."

When Tate turned back, he noticed that Dr. Niccolo had raised the pipette, and she was observing it closely.

He knew now what she was planning to do with it.

"Don't do it, Helen. We stopped your truck. None of the contaminated medicine left the lab. It's over. Just open the door."

"It doesn't matter. None of it matters." At some point, Niccolo had put down the vial and now she was gripping the two diamonds that hung on the chain around her neck. "I'll let him decide."

"No!" Tate screamed.

But it was too late.

Dr. Helen Niccolo raised the pipette and squirted its entire contents into her mouth. And then she swallowed and sat calmly on the floor.

"I'll see you soon, Jesse and Jamie. If God wills it, I will see you soon."

Chapter 39

"I'VE GIVEN YOU A HIGH dose of antiretrovirals as a precautionary measure," Dr. Mason informed Chase as she sat on the side of the bed. "But like I said, we ran RT-PCR on both blood and respiratory samples, and both came back negative for the virus. We also detected IgG antibodies in your serum, indicating that you still have some protection against the regular measles virus from the vaccine you received as a child."

Chase refrained from mentioning that Bob Santilli had also been vaccinated and his brain had swollen to the size of a watermelon.

"So, I'm clear?"

"Not exactly," Dr. Mason said, tapping a clipboard against his hand. "I'm recommending that you remain quarantined for four days, at which point we will retest you. If you're still negative then, then you'll be cleared to go."

Chase was aghast.

"Four days?"

The doctor looked at her gravely.

"I was leaning toward a week, but something tells me that you won't wait that long."

"Well, give your intuition a raise."

Dr. Mason was wearing a fitted N95 mask as well as a face shield, and he subconsciously tightened the straps on the former.

There was a knock on the window and Chase turned her eyes in that direction.

It was Tate, and he was gesturing for the doctor to come out. Like Mason, he too was wearing a mask, but his was the same one that he'd been sporting since the failed raid on the Path to Eden.

"I'll be right back."

As Dr. Mason went to converse with Tate, Chase thought back to the conversation that she'd had on the phone with her partner a few hours ago.

He'd explained what had happened, told her about Dr. Niccolo and her plan as well as her willful ingestion of the virus.

Chase had wanted to tell him then how sorry she was for what she'd said, but he didn't give her a chance.

Tate's shoulders seemed to relax in response to something Dr. Mason said. Then he shook the man's hand an absurd number of times.

The doctor pointed at her, and Tate nodded.

Moments later, her partner entered the room and approached her bed.

"I'm sorry," Chase blurted. "I don't know—I don't know why do these things. I guess—" she sighed, and condensation formed on her nose and upper lip.

Typically, this was the point when Tate would step in, say that it was all right, and tell her that he understood and that he forgave her.

Not this time.

This time, she'd gone too far.

Chase hoped that they still had a chance because she really did love him.

She looked away as she spoke.

Tate deserved the truth and that was all he ever really wanted.

"I guess… every time I'm in a situation where the risk is my life versus someone else's, someone who is innocent, I choose them over me." Chase's voice was soft, her cadence slow. She stared at her hands, flipping them over, pretending to search for a rash that wasn't there. "My sister didn't deserve to be taken and I didn't deserve to get away. I feel guilty that she went through what she did, while I got to forget and live my life. I don't deserve any of it, and I definitely don't deserve you." As she uttered this last part, Chase looked up at Tate. The sadness in his eyes reflected hers.

"You know that that wasn't your fault, right? What happened to you and Georgina? And you didn't forget, your memories were erased. That wasn't your doing, either."

"I know. But that doesn't change the facts."

"I love you, Chase," Tate said unexpectedly. "I'm not really sure why, but I do. You talk a lot about what is and isn't deserved, so let me add my opinion on the matter. I don't deserve your wrath. I've only ever tried to be good to you. I'm not perfect, far from it. But I've been honest, and I've been fair. You've been neither."

"I know." Chase took a shuddering breath. "And if you want to leave me, I understand."

Tate stiffened.

"You have to stop saying that, Chase. You keep looking for the easy way out—I'm not going anywhere."

This made Chase smile.

And then, Tate clapped his hands and started toward the door.

Chase watched him in confusion.

"Well?" Tate said, glancing over his shoulder. "You coming?"

"Where? Dr. Mason said I had to stay here for the next four days."

"You won't listen to me, but you're going to listen to some doctor?"

Chase made a face.

"I'm kidding. Mason begrudgingly said that as long as you keep your mask on, you're free to wander the hospital. Nobody is at risk. So, c'mon, let's wrap this case up once and for all."

***

With all of the kids who had been at Tyson Foods getting beds, there weren't many left for anybody else. Like Chase, they'd all gotten a clean bill of health. Dr. Mason had informed her that putting her mask on Thomas Brewer's head had probably saved his life. Unlike herself and Derek Rennick, he was unvaccinated.

But similar to Chase, they were instructed to stay put for about a week.

Ideally, Helen Niccolo, née Rennick, would have been separated from her father Derek, located at opposite ends of the hospital, maybe even on different floors.

But it was first come, first serve, and they were the last two to be admitted to Billings General.

Low priority.

The first room they came across was Helen's. She lay on the bed, eyes closed, looking completely and utterly normal.

But that was only on the outside.

On the inside, the virus was replicating at a dramatic rate.

Chase felt a familiar tightness in her stomach as she stared at the woman through the glass. If Tate hadn't been standing beside her she would have ignored it. But his presence encouraged introspection.

Chase wasn't mad that the woman had poisoned herself, that she'd taken the easy way out.

She didn't give a fuck either way.

No, what made Chase's blood boil was the fact that she hadn't been the one to bring Dr. Niccolo in. She needed to personally take down people like Helen Niccolo, like Rennick, like Delvecchio and the Jardine brothers. Tony Metcalfe, Henry Saburra, Father David, Lance O'Neill, and long before any of them, FBI Agent Chris Martinez.

The list went on and on.

She willed these feelings away.

This wasn't about her; it never had been.

It was about the kids, it was about stopping those intent on infecting the world.

And Chase had done that—no, *they* had done that.

"Dr. Mason told me that the antiretrovirals aren't enough. The viral load Dr. Niccolo swallowed was too great," Tate said.

"What's going to happen to her?"

"They're giving her drugs to stop her brain from swelling and to limit the risk of respiratory failure. But eventually, these will stop being effective. Although he didn't come out and say it, Dr. Mason hinted that Helen Niccolo probably end up like Bob Santilli."

Chase stiffened, nodded, and said, "Good."

She expected Tate to push back on this, but he didn't.

They moved to the next room which housed Derek Rennick. Unlike Helen Niccolo, he was alive and alert. He was also handcuffed to a gurney. Marshall Woods, the SWAT officer who had helped them along the way, was seated outside the room, and gave Chase a nod as they came near.

"And him?" she asked.

"He's infected, but the doc says that his viral load is much less than his daughter's. And he's been immunized, which should help. Dr. Mason thinks, but isn't sure, that Derek will recover."

"It doesn't seem fair, does it?"

"What do you mean?"

"Well, Derek Rennick is responsible for the deaths of two of his daughters. He could've gotten Jesse and Jamie vaccinated, but he didn't because of his beliefs." Chase cocked her head and reconsidered. "Scratch that, he's responsible for the deaths of *three* of his daughters. And yet, he gets to live. Like I said, it doesn't seem fair."

"It's not fair for those six boys who died, either. I don't give a shit about Bob Santilli—I'm pretty sure he knew exactly what was in the back of the truck—but those kids..."

They fell silent and Chase focused on Derek Rennick.

His lips appeared to be moving.

"What's he saying?" Chase asked.

They both put their ears against the glass.

"Let the soil beneath our feet remind us of our origins and the path we must follow. To Eden, we return, to Eden, we belong. Let the soil beneath our feet..."

"You belong in hell," Chase whispered.

"I couldn't agree more," Tate said. "Oh, I forgot to mention, the man who found the truck—Bo Kelly—is being released today. He's clean."

"Great."

"And Elijah Kane? Looks like he's gonna make a recovery, too."

"Not so great. What's going to happen to him?"

"Oh, shit, I forgot to mention, Linus called. He managed to hack into Elijah's phone. You're not going to believe this, but he was *selling* the Path to Eden land to Tyson Foods."

"What?"

"Yeah, a deal was in place, and he was the sole beneficiary. Elijah was set to make *millions*. I don't think he had an idea what was really going on with the Path to Eden, and I don't think he even cared. He was just in it for the sex and money."

"But he was their leader," Chase protested, "their figurehead. He's a piece of shit."

"I agree with that, too, but… what happens to him is in the hands of the MBI now. Because he was standing to profit from the sale of land owned by a religious institution, I have to think that at the bare minimum, he's going to be charged with some type of fraud."

It was entirely insufficient and unsatisfactory consequence for someone like Elijah.

Marshall Woods, who had been doing his best impression of a deaf-mute suddenly stood and looked past them.

Chase followed his gaze and saw Ralph Hogan and Trent Bain coming toward them.

"Shit," she murmured softly.

When Trent noticed Chase, he tried to turn back, but Ralph grabbed the man's arm.

"I'll take care of this," Tate said quietly.

"No, I will."

"I assume the fact that you're standing out here means you're safe?" Ralph Hogan said. His relief was almost palpable.

"For now—they want to keep me around for a few days to be sure."

"Glad to hear it."

Chase felt her stomach knot. This, too, she recognized.

It was pride rearing its ugly head.

She gritted her teeth.

"Agent Bain, I owe you an apology."

"As you should," Trent said sharply. "I would never jeopardize an investigation like this, half-brother, mother, father, daughter, doesn't matter. I would *never*."

Having said her piece, Chase went quiet.

Trent broke first.

"I'm glad you're okay."

"Thank you."

Keep your mouth shut, Chase, her inner voice cautioned. Yet, as Tate had succinctly pointed out, she wasn't one to heed advice.

"Just one more thing," she began, and Tate tensed.

"What?"

"Dylan Lynn Cott, you know him?"

Trent sneered.

"Yeah, a real piece of shit. Raped a young girl over a cell phone."

"What about his death?"

"What about it?"

Chase searched the man's eyes, seeking any hint of deception.

"His mother said that Dylan died under mysterious circumstances."

"Mysterious?" Trent laughed. "No mystery there. Dylan took some of the heroin that his mother had left around and shot himself in the arm. Died almost instantly."

Good enough for me, Chase thought.

Ralph cleared his throat and changed the subject.

"Good news—last shipment that left Niccolo Pharma was nearly two weeks ago. We've managed to get the serial numbers of all products that were shipped and have recalled them. We still have to test most of them, but the first few were clean. I think we're in the clear."

Chase nodded.

After an incredibly awkward pause, Trent excused himself.

"Did the MBI mention what their plan is with Natasha?"

"Agent Van Horven said that in light of the death of her three children, her charge is being downgraded from attempted murder to aggravated assault. Given the mitigating circumstances and her lack of criminal history, I don't suspect she'll get more than six months in County."

Finally, some good news.

Finally.

Ralph shook both hers and Tate's hands before he left, too.

"We should probably take you back to see Dr Mason," Tate said when it was only the two of them and the deaf-mute Marshall Woods left in the hall.

Chase recoiled.

"Why?"

"I think he made a mistake," Tate continued with a straight face. "You must be sick."

"What are you talking about? Do I have a rash? Is there something on my face?" Chase reached up and frantically touched her mask.

"No, no, nothing like that. But Chase Adams apologizing? Chase, I think you might have a head injury."

Epilogue

Two Weeks Later

"No, you don't understand. I'm having the best time—*seriously*."

Chase couldn't help but smile.

She thought back to when she'd met Rachel, and how withdrawn and pale the girl had been, alive but barely living.

But now, Rachel was vibrant, excited, everything a young girl attending college should be.

"And check this out," Rachel continued. They were standing in the center of her dorm room and with Tate, Chase, and Georgina watching, Rachel removed the straps holding her assistance poles to her arms and set them aside.

"Rachel," Tate warned.

"No, Dad, you gotta see this."

Tate tensed and held his hands out in case Rachel fell. But she didn't. The girl took three steps without any aid before stopping and bracing herself against the nearest wall.

"That's amazing!" Chase said.

Georgina clapped.

It was incredible how plastic the brain could be. As recently as ten months ago, Rachel had been confined to a wheelchair. Now, she was walking. Sure, it was only three steps, but it was a *huge* three steps.

"I know, right? I've been going to physio every day."

Chase looked in Tate's direction.

He was smiling and there were tears in his eyes.

This, in turn, made Chase beam.

They spoke for fifteen minutes, Georgina describing how her first week of high school had been, how annoying the boys were, how immature, while Rachel told them about her classes.

Chase and Tate kept their portion of the conversation brief, electing to speak about the time they spent together during the four days she was stuck in quarantine, leaving out the quarantine part.

A quick case, a much-needed vacation.

Neither was entirely untrue.

In actuality, they'd worked out many of their problems during the downtime. Chase still struggled with her inherent guilt, yet she was improving at identifying these feelings for what they truly were. Surely, that was a positive first step... wasn't it?

"All right, we should get going," Chase said when the conversation lulled.

As she spoke, she gave Georgina a nod. The girl's eyes widened before she slipped into character.

"Hey, guys, do you think it would be alright if I stayed with Rachel for the night? She could show me around campus."

Tate's mouth opened, his expression hinting at an impending objection, but Chase swiftly interjected.

"I'm okay with it."

Tate winced.

"I dunno…"

"Come on, I'll be good for them."

Tate was confused by her reaction but eventually agreed.

"It's amazing that Rachel's walking," Chase said as they got back into the car.

"I can't believe it."

Tate slid behind the wheel.

"You want to get something to eat?" Chase asked. "I'm hungry."

"Sure."

"Good, because I've picked out the perfect spot for lunch."

***

Tate wasn't stupid; when Chase suggested that they stop at the same restaurant that he'd taken her to before the call from Stitts had interrupted them, he knew something was up.

And the man was grinning from ear to ear.

The waiter came by with two glasses and filled them with champagne.

Chase instructed him to leave the bottle and she waited for the bubbles to die down before raising her glass.

"Tate, I want to thank you. I want to thank you for staying with me. I'm an asshole sometimes—" Tate raised both eyebrows. "… most the time, I guess, but I really do love you."

"Yep, you're infected. Your brain is—"

"I'm not done yet," Chase said, and Tate stopped joking. She swirled her glass, stirring up more bubbles. "I love you, and I want to marry you."

This caught Tate off guard, and she savored the moment. Few things surprised her partner anymore but this, apparently, did.

"Not today, but soon. I was thinking about a spring wedding. What do you say?"

Tate took so long to answer that Chase began to doubt herself. And then he downed his entire glass of champagne, stood up, and walked over to her.

"Get up," he instructed. Chase obliged and Tate embraced her tightly. After a moment, he pulled back and kissed her full on the lips.

"Are you sure that this—our life—will be as important to you as your work?" he asked, repeating the words that she'd used to hurt him out front of the Tyson Foods warehouse.

Chase didn't hesitate.

"Yes."

"Then I would love that." Tate hugged her again.

"Except, if you ever have me arrested again, I swear to God..."

Tate laughed.

"Alright, I won't have you arrested," he conceded, sporting a sheepish smile. "Let's get out of here; I have a different idea for how we can use those handcuffs."

END

Author's Note

YOU MIGHT BE WONDERING WHY there is no recap preceding this book, as has been my habit for the past few releases. I considered it, but it's only been a month since the last Chase book, *Tainted Blood,* was released. If you can't remember that far back, maybe you have a head injury, too—Chase Adams with an apology? *Really?* But I also wanted to keep the four-year time jump hidden for at least a chapter or two.

So, why the time jump, you ask?

It's all part of my master plan. I've labeled *Deadly Cargo* as the first book in what I'm calling Season Two for a reason. My plan is to, like Season One, have twelve 'episodes' in this season (that's my plan, but if you've been with me this long, you know how perfectly I like to stick to those).

If all goes well, Season Three will follow and it will be *very* different from Seasons One and Two. I know, I know, change is terrifying. What's that? You don't trust? Shame on you.

Trust is a powerful drug. Just ask Chase Adams.

I hope you've enjoyed this installment of Chase's tumultuous life and—wait for it, call to action incoming—if you did, please leave a brief review on Amazon. These help new readers find Chase, which, in turn, allows me to write more of her insane adventures. One last thing: don't forget to pre-order the 14th book in the series, *Active Shooter*, available soon!

As always, you keep reading and I'll keep writing.

Pat

Montreal, 2024 (←really? It's 2024 *already?*)

Printed in Great Britain
by Amazon

39346559R00128